Fragments

Fragments

John Ellison

Matador
9 Priory Business Park,
Wistow Road, Kibworth Beauchamp,
Leicestershire. LE8 0RX
Tel: 0116 279 2299
Email: books@troubador.co.uk
Web: www.troubador.co.uk/matador
Twitter: @matadorbooks

ISBN 978 1789013 504

British Library Cataloguing in Publication Data.
A catalogue record for this book is available from the British Library.

Printed and bound by 4Edge Limited
Typeset in 11pt Aldine by Troubador Publishing Ltd, Leicester, UK

Matador is an imprint of Troubador Publishing Ltd

'The past is a foreign country: they do things differently there.'

From *The Go-Between* by L.P. Hartley

This book is dedicated to Sylvia.

John Ellison is a latecomer to writing fiction, but not to thinking about doing so. His first novel (*Times Change – Before the Children Act*) was published in 2016. He writes in retirement – from lecturing in further education, and from specialism in children's law as a London solicitor, initially in local government, and, later, in the high street. He lives in Suffolk.

1

It must surely be a good moment to abandon this account of my life in London in the late nineteen sixties at the very moment I begin, and to retreat to my garden. I could crop the too-flourishing lawn, and consider dead-heading some flowers or other obvious garden care tasks. Or maybe I'll just switch the kettle on. Of course, in those far-off days, in homes like mine, anyway, a kettle was a kettle. Something to be put on, not switched on. Something to be heated above a gas burner; not something plugged in to be electrified into action. You could not take the luxury of central heating for granted either. The days of electric fires, one slim glowing bar or perhaps two (mine had been bought by me for nineteen shillings and eleven pence and did have two bars), and even the days of paraffin heaters were not over. Getting into bed to get warm was still a widespread necessity of daily life in cold weather, and you squeezed under blankets to do so. You didn't roll under a duvet, as is the custom these days for so many of us. My name, by the way, is Clive Bates.

I have, as you can see, already refused my own advice by completing a whole paragraph on my lean and neat laptop computer. Four decades ago, when I typed, I used a slim-bodied, light-blue, manual typewriter, and a copy of whatever I was typing was secured by inserting carbon paper between the two sheets that were to work their way slowly around the cylinder towards a finished condition. Mobile phones were a curse and a convenience for the distant future, while if you had a house phone – I used my landlady's occasionally – it was anchored firmly in one place. These were usually dark, funereal-looking items, mostly situated close to front doors.

And now I have completed two paragraphs. Something seems to have been decided for me. So although cancelling my volunteer writing commitment might constitute an excellent plan of action, I shall soldier on for the moment, and probably finish this chapter before taking a break, or even ending this foolishness entirely.

Acknowledgement, and without apology, must be made that almost no violence by individuals, and not much in the way of dramatic events, occur within this memoir. It is primarily an account of people and events in the east London further education college where I was employed to teach law between the autumn of nineteen sixty-eight and the spring of the following year. My immediate environment was remarkably civilised, calm and protected, although my head was never quite free of troubles outside it, such as large-scale planned death and devastation taking place in distant countries.

Another admission. To the best of my knowledge the celebrity magazines have never spoken of any of the principal actors, and I do not expect any would wish to write about any of us after reading this story, or, more accurately, this collection of stories. These repeatedly interrupted chronicles are no more than slices of ordinary lives, fragments of lives; small fragments I have now, more than forty years later, through memory entered again.

At that time I kept a journal, writing up trivia and trivia-plus conscientiously every day or two. I did not make the effort to read this banal collation again until last spring, when, conscientiously, I set about an exploration of ancient accumulated papers, throwing out what I felt I could liberate myself from without pain or sadness. Over the years I had not forgotten the existence of this messy record of events, just noting its presence in a crammed drawer from time to time, leaving re-acquaintance with its tedious 'secrets' to a rainier day.

The temptation to revisit my diary had from time to time risen up, but in response I feared that if I did so, I would be compelled to read all of it, probably an emotional as well as a time-consuming business. So across the years it remained untouched. Then last spring, as I say, sitting in my chair in my small book-lined study, with a steaming cup of coffee to my right hand, I began to read this long abandoned scribble. And sat up late to do so, coffee almost entirely forgotten. Very late.

The journey through the diary was disturbing: marked by so many discoveries of forgotten moments, as well as by the most yawn-invoking of entries. Though the content was selective, and skipped details which flew out at me from stored memory, it brought back potently a real sense of my life then. It brought to trembling reality, far more amply than I had imagined, the people with whom I was rubbing shoulders in and away from the college which employed me. There were names mentioned to which I could not now put either faces or personality, though these forgotten labels belonged only to the outermost margins of the story that was, as I read on, retold. I was reminded powerfully of the difficulties which seemed to have no end in the lives of two of my colleagues, and of the eruption of little and larger crises that took place in my assigned college department. These episodes produced short-lived flames which seemed to illuminate brightly the positions and preferences of some individuals who will appear in due course. That is, if I decide to carry through the project.

Physically, my journal consisted of two small but thick notebooks (secured by a tired and deteriorated elastic band), filled with rushed, often semi-legible handwriting, and containing far more information than I had expected to be concealed there. It refreshed my memory with stunning force. And because it was written in a different time, with the knowledge, mental assumptions, inclinations and ignorance which were mine (though hardly exclusively), I was enabled from afar to view those days in a way not contemporaneously possible. Time and I had moved on.

Some omissions from my diary back-handed me in the face. I had recorded so much routine, so much mundaneness, but I had not recorded much involvement on my part with events taking place in the wider world, for the unanswerable reason that my involvement in these was very slight indeed. I shuddered when I considered the possibility that a nuclear war might devastate the world, but tried to put the thought out of mind. I did little more than sigh over the daily slaughter of the American war in Vietnam, and over the absence of condemnation of that war by Britain's Labour government of the time (and the Conservative Parliamentary Opposition). I had greeted with contained curiosity the student uprising in France in May, as final examinations stepped up to me. Through reading newspapers I limply registered early signals of coming catastrophe in Northern Ireland; and at a time of lively price inflation, while trade unions were bombarded with blame from Labour and Conservatives alike for industrial conflict, and were subjected to proposals for controlling and penalising them, I was just another bystander. But not everyone around me was as disengaged from public debate as I was, as my notebooks reminded me.

These modest archives started to tell me, collectively, that I should write up the story as fully and engagingly as I could. On the other hand, 'engagingly' might not prove to be very engaging at all. So I should perhaps stop right here. If I cease writing now, I could certainly do something plainly constructive. If I ignore my small garden, I could do useful things in the house, now at last mortgage-free.

Enough of dithering. I shall carry on, for the time being

at least, with putting words to paper in these final months of the year 2010, when on Britain's high streets evidence of economic recession is difficult to overlook, and when the policies of a miserly and oppressive new government circle above us. I can't quite get those long disappeared times of my early adulthood out of mind, even though they were hardly crammed with peril or devilment, and I have an increasing desire to write about them.

At least perfunctory scene-setting is called for, and I answer the call. Done with university, I was without appetite for any employment that implied serious industry or serious money. The owner of a law degree (a certificate, Jack O'Neill was to tell me, that confirmed I was an accredited member of the middle class), I had settled on teaching my subject to young people in a so-called technical college. That is, if one would have me. And have me, one did, thankfully without excessive effort in exchange on my part.

East Ham Technical College was positioned in not very pretty and not very prosperous suburban east London, not quite as far out on the district tube line as Barking. My route there for a job interview on a sunny summer afternoon (from a one bedroom rented furnished flat in a side street off the Holloway Road), took me to East Ham underground station, from which a few minutes' walk along the lengthy High Street led me to my destination.

The main building was colourless cheap modern and of seven floors, and was linked to a much older, modestly sized annexe across the road, tucked behind the still imposing dark red brick Town Hall. This, dating back to circa 1900, still continued to play its municipal role.

After this introduction, the door must open to this account of a fragment of my life, and of fragments of the lives of others.

2

My working life at the college started on a dull day in early September when staff were directed to attend, without the distraction of a student presence, in order to prepare for the battles to come. Arriving early and anxiously, I decided to use up waiting time in the little café across the road from the annexe building nudging the Town Hall. There was a sprinkling of square tables, each with its own lemon-coloured plastic table-cloth, decorated with salt and pepper pots, and a large white sugar shaker. A tallish man was already at the counter, ordering coffee in a well-spoken voice, and I waited for him to be served. Fixed up myself soon with a cup of tea, I hesitated as to where to sit, but then saw that my fellow customer had put on the wall-adjacent table in front of him the college brochure which I had also been sent in the post and asked to bring on this day. I put my own copy of the brochure and my tea on his table, and asked if he minded my occupying one of the vacant chairs. I immediately received a friendly greeting.

'Snap,' he said. 'You must be one of us.' His face was suddenly full of sunshine if not hilarity.

'Business Studies?' I asked him, for the annexe building near to us was much occupied by this subject area.

'Business and General Studies,' he said, accenting the 'General'. 'The concepts of business and commerce snap at you like alligators from a swamp. I prefer to think of myself as more of a General Studies person. I teach English. My first term here.'

'Mine too,' I said. I had been sizing him up more closely. He had penetrating blue eyes, dishevelled and disappearing hair, and seemed enormously at ease. His sports jacket was well-worn, his collar frayed, and his tie had less colour than had been once the case. I was taken aback by one aspect of his dress – his rumpled and ageing corduroy trousers were secured at the waist by a length of rope with frayed ends. As we spoke he had been fiddling with the rope ends. Aware I was examining his trouser security arrangements, he explained without embarrassment that he hadn't been able to find a belt that morning.

'I make a point of being a parody of a respectably dressed person. I'm Jack O'Neill.'

He looked at me with more attention than previously. I was wearing a new pinstripe suit (with a matching waistcoat) and was moderately proud of it, while my savage short back and sides' haircut and sober tie were conspicuous features. I was registering his perceptible, but qualified, Irish accent.

'Clive Bates,' I said. 'I teach law. Or at least I shall be doing so shortly.'

'Your outfit is enough corroboration of that for me,' he said. 'You have the appearance of a minor public school tyke.' This was said in meditative fashion, but not unkindly. Amused, I asked him how he liked the idea of teaching at this establishment. He had no difficulty in providing an answer:

'Teaching a class of pretty girls about erotic references in the poems of John Donne and being paid for it is in my view a reasonable way of making a living.'

'And what about the people you will be working with?'

'They're all right. This is my first term. I was teaching in a school before. That saga ended in total disaster. If I hadn't given in my notice, I'm sure they'd have got rid of me. I expect the same will happen here. At some moment soon, chaos will erupt, the roof will fall in and I'll be on the road again, returning like an old tramp to the Embankment. As in the Flanagan and Allen song. *Underneath the Arches*. You know it?'

All this flowed out of him with a mix of cheerfulness and resignation. I could see this conversation might become protracted, and was keeping an eye on my watch.

'Do you have English-teaching colleagues?' I asked.

'Two,' he said. 'We're a Welshman – that's Oliver Price – and an Englishman (and he's very English) – that's Peter Dawlish – and an Irishman. That's me. Jack O'Neill. Oh, yes. I think we have another colleague – for half the time, anyway. Someone called Shirley. I'm already dreaming about Shirley, probably because I haven't met her yet.'

I introduced myself again, and more fully, though strongly suspected after doing so that he had not yet inscribed my name in his memory. He looked to me as if he was thinking, with concern, about something quite different. I put out my hand, which he shook after a moment. 'Your handshake matches your suit,' he threw in.

'Time to go over the road,' I proposed. Suddenly possessed with edgy panic, he looked desperately at his watch, was reassured by what he saw, and solemnly agreed. So across the road we went, taking advantage of a short-lived space between rapidly and noisily moving vehicles.

As we walked I made an effort to hold in my mind the names of the English-teaching trio: Oliver Price, Peter Dawlish, Jack O'Neill, plus a half-timer called Shirley. I needn't have bothered with concentration. I met the first two, but not Shirley, later that day. Once encountered, their individual identities were fixtured in my head.

3

I now travel back in time a few weeks to offer some more context to my first days at the college. My interview for the vacant law lecturer post had been in the main high street building, and had not needed significant preparation or anxious nail-biting. Offering to teach law, as I was, on the sole basis of my scraped honours degree in the subject, equipped with absolutely no training in teaching, and the most abysmal ignorance of the realities of the legal and commercial world, I was nevertheless in a strong bargaining position for this junior role.

Few others whom I knew to be in a situation similar to mine wished to pass up rather better paid legal practice or commercial opportunities, and there were more than enough openings of that sort for those tempted. There was even the option of the Civil Service, but I was not envious of a fellow graduate acquaintance, just recruited by her Majesty, who had told me that in the office he had joined, his immediate superior expected to be addressed as 'Sir'. Indeed, this expectation had been underlined by 'Sir' having affixed little notes at strategic points around and about, such as 'Sir's Filing Cabinet', 'Sir's Desk' and 'Sir's In-Tray'.

Obviously teaching of some sort was for me. I was one of only two interviewed candidates for a post at East Ham as the summer vacation was beginning, and I wondered about the chances of the other male candidate as I watched him and spoke to him in the ante-room, before being called in.

He was black, Nigerian I supposed, friendly and intelligent to judge from my short conversation with him, but he definitely lacked a white British accent, and all of the teaching staff I had seen, during an early recce, were white. Of course, I could be wrong in my youthful guesswork, but I was the one who was to fill the vacancy, and he didn't, after facing three white male members of the interviewing panel. Perhaps I had better qualifications than he had. Or similar. Or worse.

The Principal, a thin, tall man of around sixty with the surname of Plummer, was flanked by two others (whom he did not trouble to introduce) to make up the panel, and my short and formal interview took place in his ground floor office. He asked me a few questions which contained no surprises and reflected no exercise of imagination, while I tried to make my answers coherent, yet having a vague sense that I was talking in my sleep. The other panel members stayed silent, neither smiling nor scowling. One of these, well into his fifties, had a round, benign face and a head that was entirely bald. The other, perhaps two decades younger, was a man with less distinctive features, but who during the interview shifted about restlessly in his chair.

I was asked to wait, waited, and was soon afterwards invited in again to be offered the post. Immediately after saying yes (with a smile of gratitude which I tried, probably unsuccessfully, to make polite instead of joyous), I was shown around the premises by my predecessor in the post. He was the younger of the two silent men on the panel whose not sitting still I had noticed. He now presented himself as genial and indiscreet as well as mobile. He told me frankly he had used the college blatantly as a jumping-off point for securing a lecturing spot in a Polytechnic somewhere up north. He would henceforth be teaching degree students. He rattled on, without giving me much chance to ask questions, but I felt no need to do so anyway.

I was shown the library, and the characterless and uninhabited staff common room, in the modern building. After that we crossed the road to the Town Hall, whose straight and gloomy corridor took us eventually into open air. Close ahead of us then was the old building annexe. Inside this were more corridors, set in the shape of a square. We inspected the dirty pink walled annexe staff common room in one corner. This had a friendlier feel than that in the main block, though it, too, was devoid of a human presence. The upright chairs and softer armchairs (there were more of the former than the latter) certainly looked lived in.

In another corner of this old building I was to have the use of a desk, and some almost empty book shelves behind glass, in a much smaller room which also had dirty pink walls. This room, I was told, I would share with two colleagues. It was, in effect, my office. After rather less than a minute, my companion, who had been tapping one of his feet impatiently on the floor, turned to leave the room. I followed him obediently.

'I expect you'll be teaching in the annexe most of the time,' he said. 'It's more homely here than over the road.'

Back in the larger staff room he gestured towards the wooden pigeon-hole repository for class registers, and warned me that the only real crime thereabouts was to lose a register or not fill it up conscientiously with names, ticks, crosses and totals. 'Fill in registers well and teach to a mediocre level, and they'll know you're one of them,' he said.

'Is it conceivable,' I asked boldly, 'that you're an old cynic?'

He laughed, didn't answer, and then mimicked vividly a 'register fiend' in the Department, Reg somebody, but known to some behind his back as 'Mr. Register', a person in charge of municipal accountancy day release courses, and who gave high importance to impeccable register maintenance, questioning closely teachers contributing to these courses who failed to adhere to his own high standards.

My predecessor began the impersonation of 'Mr. Register' (cruelly attributing a harsh, shrill voice to his victim). 'Now then, Mr. X, I've entered in the register one of the students attending between nine and ten on the 20th of March, and you've recorded him as absent between ten and eleven, although he was present again for another class between eleven fifteen and twelve. That's unlikely to be right, isn't it? Could it be you made a register entry error?'

The last three words of this presentation, uttered by the man I was replacing, were pronounced slowly and with unctuous emphasis, rather like protracted chords on a church organ, and were followed by a bray of manic laughter, suddenly shut off. He became immediately restive again. I was beginning to dislike the impersonator as much as I was entertained by him.

I was later briefed about the unfamiliar courses I'd be concerned with, and I boned up somewhat on what I needed to know and deliver to students. Then in September, soon after the first 'staff only' day when I met Jack O'Neill, enrolment of students started, and from that moment I was on the treadmill. Well, a treadmill of sorts. There wasn't too much treading to do.

Perhaps I should add, some blank pages now having been littered with words, that I have decided to continue this story fiercely and relentlessly to its wretched end. I make no excuses. Those who wish to read no more do not need my permission to make an exit right here.

4

I must address the 'staff only day', which had begun with my café meeting with Jack O'Neill. It continued with a congregation of Business and General Studies staff in the main annexe staff room. The meeting was to be led by the Department's Head, Mr. Pringle. I sat down near Jack O'Neill. After later comers had entered, all chairs having been taken, several staff were left standing against the walls. I counted half a dozen women, and twice, perhaps more, that number of men. Before Mr. Pringle arrived I got up and made myself known to the Deputy Head, who had been pointed out to me. This was a white toothed, smiley, narrow-faced man, slight of build, and with a laugh far too loud for his light frame, and far too loud to sound genuine. From the first I decided he was not entirely, if at all, to be trusted. His name was Fawcett and he told me to call him David, while referring to Pringle without hesitation as 'Mr. Pringle'.

Mr. Pringle, it seemed, was by established custom not to be addressed by his first name, and this was made easier by denying advertisement of it. I remembered him, when he arrived in the staff room, as the round-faced panel member who had wordlessly interviewed me some weeks before. He had, besides a bald head, a wide, innocent smile, and gaps between his small, slightly protruding teeth. He took his place next to David Fawcett and addressed us. 'Ladies and gentlemen,' he began.

The meeting chiefly concerned practical arrangements

for the launch of the new academic year, and progressed at a very slow speed indeed. It was, even for me, a novice and a newcomer, unutterably tiresome, and I will dart forward to lunch-time. I had been told that lunch at a subsidised price was available for us on a daily basis in the first floor Town Hall canteen, and made my way there. I gravitated towards a table where Jack O'Neill was sitting, and asked if he would mind if I occupied the seat next to him.

'Ah, the lawyer,' he said. 'You won't pick up too many fees in these parts. Perhaps you'll pick up girls instead.'

'That's a very naughty thing to say.' A broad-faced, broad-shouldered and broad-stomached man of around forty, who was sitting opposite us, smiled in my direction as he spoke and introduced himself as Oliver Price.

'Oliver is our leader, first among equals,' said Jack O'Neill.

Price, who had already consumed his main course, spoke slowly, deliberately, interrupting himself occasionally with puffs at a Capstan Full Strength cigarette in a rich, fruity voice.

'I hope you'll find your stay with us comfortable,' he said courteously.

'I'm sure it will be as you hope,' I said mechanically.

Much later, Jack summed up Oliver Price to me as a slow moving and essentially well-intentioned Welshman. That was a fair description as far as it went, but proved not to be comprehensive. He had more of a BBC than a Welsh accent, encouraging the idea – which time was to reinforce – that his Welsh origin was for him not much more than a formality, and that he considered himself at least an honorary member of the English gentry.

I looked at Price's table neighbour, guessing correctly that this was Peter Dawlish. He was small in stature and probably in his late twenties. He was adorned with a black bow tie decorated with white spots, cordoned off by a wine-coloured corduroy jacket, and he soon found an opportunity to say that he had read English at Oxford. I came quickly to think of him as Bow Tie. He was the only teacher decorated in that fashion in the department, and probably in the college. At least, I thought, he didn't have the word 'Oxford' sewn neatly on to the tie.

'I'm wondering,' I said, 'if you could be Peter Dawlish.'

'I certainly couldn't be anyone else,' was the answer that came back in a confident voice.

'And don't you have another English teaching person.'

'Oh yes, Oliver Price here.'

'I mean in addition to the three of you here?'

'Oh yes, there is Shirley, Shirley Tait. She teaches half English, half Liberal Studies. An odd combination. And she's the department's trade union rep. If you're in danger of disciplinary measures, she'll make you feel safer. Perhaps. Are you in trouble yet?'

Bow Tie had assumed a mock-solicitous facial expression. I passed over his question.

'Was she at this morning's meeting?' I asked.

'Oh yes.'

'I've met her now,' said Jack O'Neill. 'And I shall continue to dream about her now I've met her. And I may get myself deliberately into trouble in order to be defended by her.'

It was at this first lunch gathering that I asked questions about Mr. Pringle, how long he'd been head of department and so forth. Bow Tie responded crisply and immediately.

'He's all right,' he said. 'Doesn't interfere. Lets us get on with it. They appointed him unanimously by all accounts. The governors, that is. That was last year. He's a friend of Reg, the register fiend. Have you heard about Reg?'

Discussion about Mr. Register, of whom I had heard enough already, was nipped in the bud. 'Mr. Pringle is,' said Oliver Price, inhaling deeply on his cigarette, 'whatever anyone else might say, a gentleman.'

This was said with warmth. Mr. Pringle does not play

a major part in this bundle of tales, but I might as well say something more about him on the basis of my later experience.

I have already mentioned his round face, his teeth and his baldness. He was also a cautious, staid but kindly man. He was markedly less authoritarian in style than his necessarily female secretary, who liked to refer to him in a tone of voice which emphasised impressively his senior managerial status. I didn't see a lot of him in the months to come except when I wanted supplies of stationery. The allocation and distribution of paper was not a task he felt he could safely delegate. He doled it out sparingly, first unlocking with care the store room door, and then a stationery cupboard inside. It was all done with an element of painful reluctance, as if he had, against his better judgment, taken another small but definite pace down a road leading inexorably towards the bankruptcy and dissolution of the college. He mostly hid in his room, the convenient L-shape of which suited his wish as far as possible to avoid being observed.

For a minute or two there was silence at our table while eating, and in Oliver Price's case, while smoking, continued. To quell the quietness, and from frank curiosity, I asked Jack O'Neill what he had meant when he referred earlier to a total disaster at the secondary school where he had been teaching before he had taken up this present post.

'I shouldn't be proud of it,' he said. 'It was one of my little faux pas, a most unfortunate development which should have led to my being scrapped. There is a history of such incidents involving me.'

'Yes?'

'I was once acting head master at a private school, not a large one. About one hundred and fifty boys. The head was sick and so were several more senior staff, so I was left in charge. There was complete mayhem.'

'You mean you're not famous for firm and decisive

leadership and the enforcement of discipline in a school environment?'

'In any environment, but especially in schools.'

'So what happened?'

"Well, I was supposed to read grace at meal-times. I would get out the words: 'For what we have to receive,' and my voice would start to crack with suppressed laughter, and in short order there was shrieking merriment. For the rest of my tenure the boys were doing pretty much as they liked. I was half-expecting one to come up to me and say: 'I suppose it's all right to bring women in?'"

He spoke expansively and with unconfined delight in his own words, sunlight in his face. He dabbed at his mouth from time to time with a ragged paper handkerchief. I offered him a clean and intact paper substitute, which he politely accepted.

I was about to renew my question about the disaster that had occurred during Jack's final weeks at his last post, but at that moment Oliver Price, who had been exchanging thoughts on the literature syllabus with Bow Tie while I conversed with Jack, looked up and I was distracted by his observation.

'There goes the Major,' he gestured slightly towards a small, neat, suited, military looking figure who was striding towards the canteen exit. 'He seems to have recovered from the end of summer term celebrations.' Price followed this with a sustained head-shaking grin, then stubbing out his much-enjoyed cigarette.

'The Major runs management studies,' said Bow Tie. The Irishman added: 'I've been told he had a skinful on the last day of term and was sick in the piano in the hall. You could call it a piano solo of a special kind. Someone had left the lid up and the whole lot went in. I've heard that the middle C sounds more off-key than it did previously.'

A grimace from Bow Tie accompanied this piece of recent military biography followed by his glance at Jack O'Neill and a weary comment: 'You're repeating what I told you less than an hour ago.'

'At least I repeated it accurately.'

I pause here to say that during my time at the college, the Major was frequently seen approaching or departing briskly, maintaining a certain military distance from the rest of us. It was said of him that he ingested alcohol in quantities, especially but not exclusively at the ends of terms. The piano performance, I was told on this occasion (apparently on good but second hand authority), was not his first in the genre: he had done exactly the same thing on his last day at his previous college. So, it seemed, at least twice a suffering piano in a college hall had received his compliments from deep within him. If this could be believed.

'Such occurrences,' Jack O'Neill went on to declare sagely, 'are often in a sequence of three.' The third such occasion was awaited.

Management studies, the Major's allocated teaching territory, was not an area in which I was required to contribute much as a law teacher. The college balanced the provision of advanced general certificate of education subjects (leading to possible, but statistically improbable, university entrance), with lower level courses for those aspiring to back office employment in industry and trade. My own contributions were to be spread mainly between full-time sixteen and seventeen year-olds signed on for the basic ordinary national diploma in business studies, one day a week day-release students doing a broadly equivalent course, and youthful clerks in solicitors' offices who committed half a day weekly to first-stage legal studies. Then there were the rudiments of commercial law for junior staff in local authority finance departments. It was hum-drum awfulness, perhaps, for Jack O'Neill, but I did not personally feel in the least patronising about either the role of the teachers or the ambitions of the students.

The target at the end of the academic year was always an examination, in some cases set independently of the college, in others set internally by us, subject to external monitoring. I was informed by Bob Hardy, a colleague I have not yet introduced, and whose teaching speciality was 'government', that such monitoring was supplied by 'some old fool in need of beer money'.

For my own subject, I had acquired relevant text books and was to devote much time to preparing written summary material to be handed out periodically to students. Such aids to learning were reproduced by myself and my colleagues in numbers through a primitive (by today's criteria) duplicating machine with a turning handle, to which staff had ready access.

But paper itself was rationed. Obtaining paper for processing through the machine required a specific written request, with a supporting reason, to Mr. Pringle. Although requests were generally granted, Pringle would grant them with implicit regret, and on the basis that the minimum necessary paper quantity required would be issued. A class of fifteen students justified the issue of sixteen sheets of paper at most, one for the teacher and the rest for the students.

'For Mr. Pringle,' sighed Oliver Price, tapping ash neatly into a tray at his elbow from a replacement cigarette (after further desultory conversation on this 'staff only' day), 'war-time restrictions and austerity have never ended. He probably still has baths in water no deeper than five inches as insisted upon by regulations in those rationing years.'

5

I should mention that I had been appointed as one of two new junior law lecturers, the other appointee being female. She had been interviewed a few days before me, and I did not set eyes on her until the first staff preparation day I have been describing. She was quite striking from a physical point of view. Of a similar age to me, she displayed large amounts of long, straight dark hair, worn loose, and additionally possessed a voluptuous body, rosebud lips, a straight, uncomplicated nose and, frequently, a faint smile. Her name was Ann Feldman. On that first day she did not join me at my lunch table with the English teachers. She was sitting by herself not far away, and it was Oliver Price who identified her for me, nobody having introduced us at the staff meeting addressed by Mr. Pringle.

Before I left the Town Hall refectory, I went over to correct the omission. Ann Feldman smiled vaguely, and said little, as if she was thinking of something else while I told her who I was. I had a sense, after that introduction, that she was either unusually reserved or, perhaps, had worries on her mind.

That afternoon, stationed in the little pink walled staff room for three that I was to share with Ann and Ann's rather ubiquitous perfume (plus a third colleague I had not yet met), the two of us conversed more. After a few cautious exchanges she became remarkably open.

'I don't feel like a lawyer,' she volunteered. 'I don't feel I know any law.' I registered this without comment.

'I need to know some family law, though,' she went on: 'I'm going to get divorced.'

She was making a plain statement, but gave no sign that she would welcome comment or commiseration. I didn't like to probe her personal life at that moment. Embarrassed by the sudden disclosure, I allowed her words to drip on me like light, only mildly inconvenient, rain. After a few moments I asked her about her allocated timetable, which she said she couldn't find. I suggested we might be able to help each other by sharing stencilled handout notes to the students. Ann didn't seem hugely interested in the tasks ahead of us and abruptly changed the subject.

'There may not be much point in working,' she said. 'Did you know about the meteorite that's coming towards the earth? Someone told me about it. I think it's going to destroy the world.'

I looked at her more closely, wondering if she was being frivolous, but there was no sign she was.

'You don't think nuclear war is a more likely way of finishing us all off?'

Ann was flat in her reply. 'There's that too,' she said. 'I've got to go,' and she did. Her perfume stayed, and was noticed minutes later by the third of the trio of teachers who had a home base in this little room, and who now joined me.

'What a stink!' Stanley Payne said quietly, but with disgust.

This was a man with thinning light brown hair and in his mid-forties. He eased himself into his chair and leaned back in it, putting one hand and wrist well inside his trouser waist band for, it appeared, personal comfort. He told me his name and that he taught commercial subjects, mainly accountancy.

'You'll be OK here,' he said. 'Your predecessor didn't set much of an example. He spent the bulk of his time sending in job applications. A man in a hurry. Never still.'

I simulated professional disapproval by raising my eyebrows and listened for more.

'Surely he did other things as well?'

'He was a very good mimic,' said Stanley. 'Prime Ministers a speciality. He could do a marvellous Winston Churchill impersonation. Or a Harold Macmillan. The students liked him for that. He certainly wasn't over-dedicated to teaching. Gave them notes to read while he concentrated on chasing Polytechnic and University posts. Until he got one eventually.'

'I heard him mimic someone called Mr. Register,' I said neutrally. 'Oh Reg,' said Stanley. 'There's nothing much wrong with Reg. He's very conscientious, that's all. Not everyone round here is impressed by that.'

He moved on easily to another topic, his voice quiet, measured, colourless, uttering his thoughts in a resigned way.

'I hope your colleague Mrs. Feldman will fit in; I've got a feeling she may struggle. Trouble with women, of course, if it's not the time of the month, it's the menopause.'

He had introduced a theme to which he was to return a number of times over the months ahead.

'Or a plethora of perfume,' I added, neither pleased with what he had said nor brave enough at that instant to speak up for Ann or women in general.

He went on to follow further his line of thought, to say more about Ann.

'She was wearing a very revealing dress today,' he said. 'I didn't know they made skirts that short. I asked her about it and she said her mother had made it. What can you say?'

He smiled, but his smile was not quite one of forgiveness.

That episode largely concluded my initial contact with colleagues before students arrived on enrolment day. It gave me a taste of what was to come.

6

Student enrolment day. Outside, sun and an almost cloudless sky. An untidy occasion. Day students arriving and queuing up in the morning, hundreds of them. Evening class students doing the same in the evening, hundreds of them. We, the teaching staff, were scattered about in various rooms in the big building, waiting for customers to appear and enrol for the year. As a newcomer, I was given only minor tasks, while selected staff who knew what was on offer at the college were able to give accurate answers to enquiries, and send students in the right direction, such as to the correct enrolment room, or even to a different college.

I learnt that day that our establishment was situated about half-way geographically between other colleges at Barking and West Ham, and was also about half-way between these rival set-ups in academic status. West Ham supplied the lowest grade courses, we the median level, and Barking offered services a rung or two higher. Casual staff talk told me that West Ham wanted to take away our higher grade work, while we naturally favoured both keeping it and pirating as much of Barking's elite status for ourselves as we could. Though in practice, it was ruminatively said by veterans, nothing ever changed.

I listened to a question and answer between a young black man, who asked about the availability of higher national certificate courses, and a white teacher in her fifties who was memorable for an old-young china doll face, and a precise and piercing voice which evidenced that she had received elocution training at some remote stage in her past life.

'Higher national certificate?' she questioned. 'We don't do that here. Did you think you were at Barking?'

In her mind, perhaps all students were children, who needed to be reminded where they were at any given time. So I imagined tolerantly. But black students (in those days usually termed by the press, TV and white people like me as coloured) were, I suspected, in her sub-conscious people map, even more like children than the others.

The seriousness of the enrolment exercise didn't prevent a few staff members from sidling off when they felt their presence could be dispensed with. In the early evening, after the first rush of evening attenders was digested and distributed, and the inwards flow had diminished, Peter Dawlish – he of English and Bow Tie studies – came over.

'What about a drink?' he proposed. We headed out of the tall building and made for the Denmark Arms, which was situated on one corner of the junction from which the road to Barking ran west, and the High Street led northwards to the underground railway station. This was a traditional English pub with a fairly elaborate turn of century exterior and a large saloon bar. The architecture seemed to me to be compatible with, and even similar to, that of the nearby Town Hall. Already a few teachers were present. I caught sight of the Irishman, Jack O'Neill, waving a pound note at a barmaid and failing to be served, while Peter Dawlish squeezed to the front, and effortlessly acquired halves of bitter for the two of us. He lit up a pipe and began to reminisce about my law teaching predecessor. 'I expect you're more conventional,' he said, taking a puff from his pipe. 'Our colleagues didn't take to him, but he had abilities.'

'I've heard he applied for a lot of jobs.'

Said Dawlish: 'A lot of us do that. He was just more public

about it. He also took a few risks. Did you know he was rather good at mimicry?'

'I've heard that too.'

"Well, he could do Max Miller. You know: 'When apples are ripe they are ready for plucking. When girls are sixteen…'"

As he spoke, Dawlish distanced himself by his manner from the muckiness of the humour to which he was referring, preferring, it seemed, to wear the mask of a man of the world with patient tolerance of the more vulgar amusements of others.

'He even tried it out on a mixed class. Nobody reported him. But he was taking a chance, I'd say. Not cut out for teaching though. Not here, anyway. A man in a hurry.' He waved his pipe good-naturedly.

'How would you describe the atmosphere here,' I asked. 'Old-fashioned? Fuddy duddy? Square? Not 'with it'?'

'You've got it in four,' said Peter Dawlish, who had evidently been counting my list of options. 'Some are more old-world than others. For instance there's a staff-instigated bible fellowship group meeting once a week. Reg, the register fiend, runs that. You can see the notice about it on the board. Mind you, I don't think it's exactly a mass meeting. Pringle participates occasionally, I'm told, though he doesn't like leaving his office. My English teaching partner Oliver Price – head of English, you know, approves of stability, continuity, tradition. You might consider him old-fashioned. The idea of a bible class may appeal to him in principle, but the idea of actually attending doesn't. I think Oliver's agnostic in religion, but not about tradition. I'm a convinced agnostic myself.'

'Old-world too?' I dared to ask, of this bow tie'd creature who was probably only a year or so older than I was.

'Why not,' he replied.

'No compulsory morning prayers for all staff then,' I pronounced as if relieved.

I brought up that I had not yet met his colleague Shirley Tait. Peter Dawlish responded instantly: 'Well, you're missing something. She was on liberal studies duty this evening. You can rely on Shirley to be where she should be.'

At that moment Jack O'Neill joined us. He had finally got himself a pint, though had spilt some of it retreating clumsily from the bar. He sank into a chair. 'I shouldn't really be here,' he said. 'I should be on my way home to a row.'

He looked gloomy, anxious.

'Not marital bliss at home?' I queried. 'Wait till you're married,' he said. 'In my experience, not long after the wedding the woman goes mad.'

This certainly suggested a different approach to thinking about women than I had collected from Stanley Payne.

With little prompting, and cheering up, Jack O'Neill now gave us – though I supposed Peter Dawlish might have heard it before – a few more details of his recent life history. He had, prior to his entry into further education at this college, been teaching at a succession of inner London secondary schools. He had not found the life easy. He found keeping order in the classroom an impossible task, and that teaching became a realistic proposition only if he had the headmaster in the room with him. He would teach; the headmaster would control. Jack's wife Sally created additional problems, by getting into screaming rows with people she met, or interfering with public order at the schools which employed him to teach.

'Sally is fundamentally insane,' he said 'and spends a good deal of her time in the madhouse.'

'I'm sorry about that,' I said weakly.

At one place where he had taught, he said, she had come into the school playground, riding a bicycle; and at break-time, when Jack, having been advised of her presence, had emerged from the building, she had chased him back inside, dumping the bicycle desperately to pursue him on foot. She would repeatedly accuse him publicly of having affairs with schoolgirls. Life hadn't been totally devoid of moments of interest, he summed up with a rueful grin.

'On the other hand, I've gathered I'm not the only one in this staff room with marital troubles,' he went on.

While Jack O'Neill was regaling me with this information, Peter Dawlish, so much nearer my own age, while having the demeanour of a middle aged man, was conversing with his pipe and looking meditative. Jack fastened kindly eyes on him.

'You're not married yet, are you?' he said.

Said Dawlish, reluctant for his private life to be illuminated, limiting his response: 'That's entirely correct.'

'If I want to go out somewhere by myself,' said Jack, 'I have to give Sally at least a month's notice. Even then, she's likely to try to sabotage it. Do you get out much?' he asked Peter.

'Oh, sometimes on a Saturday evening we go out for a meal and do a show. But I must be off now. Need my beauty sleep.'

And he went, nodding polite farewells in our direction. I learnt later that he lived some way out of London, and had a fiancée who worked in a merchant bank.

Jack resumed his account of his life situation. 'I've got a kid. Thomas. Aged three. One reason why I have to get back home is that she keeps him up till eleven at night, and she doesn't pay much attention to him. She's just been let out of hospital.'

'How long had she been there?'

'Three days. She was shouting racialist abuse,' he said, 'at some West Indians in the street. They beat her up and the police were called. They took her to hospital. She was slapped in a padded cell and given an injection.'

'And she's out now?' I was trying to keep up with all this lurid information.

'Since last night. This morning,' he went on, emphasising

his words, 'She's off to Westminster to find the Home Secretary, James Callaghan. She wants to get a written guarantee from him that she won't be picked up again by the police, on the grounds that the Attorney-General is the brother-in-law of a friend of hers. She's got the kid with her.'

This had been said with harsh fluency, but with a quality of sadness too. I shook my head inwardly at the crisis-ridden existence led by Jack – and by little Thomas and his mother. Jack, I discovered then, took the same train route as I was taking between college and home. One stop on the district line to Barking, then the east-west overland line to Upper Holloway. He took a bus from there, while I lived a short walk southwards from the station. We travelled homewards together that evening, chatting, though his share of the speaking was much larger than mine.

Jack told me more about his past. He had once been a public lavatory attendant, and had become angry whenever his handiwork was befouled. When he had cleaned throughout and everything was shining bright, he couldn't bring himself to make use of his own spotless facilities, and darted round the corner into a public house toilet for the necessary personal relief.

He had also, he said, once been a hack journalist. This had been in Dublin, soon after he had left school. Once he had written up, he thought, in fine style, the Corpus Christi festival – describing the street procession in the sun and so forth. Unfortunately he had committed the piece to paper before the procession set out, and it so happened that a sudden violent downpour had cancelled the mass promenade. By the time Jack found out, it was too late to stop the article appearing. Everyone laughed so much, he said, that they forgot to fire him.

'I got into the limelight again,' he continued, 'reporting football matches. My interest in football was absolutely nil, and during most of the play I was in the bar. Tragically I couldn't get the score right, so I was taken off sports reporting altogether.'

I was listening keenly, as the train rolled on, enlivened by Jack's anecdotage.

'But what exactly,' I asked, reviving the topic by-passed by him in an earlier conversation, 'was the catastrophe you started to tell me about in the café at your last secondary school?'

'Telling you about it,' he admitted, 'doesn't, I think, set me off to the best advantage.'

'Please proceed, though.'

'It was in a drama class,' he said. 'Fourteen-year-olds, a mixed class. There wasn't a problem at first.'

'But what transpired?'

'I asked three girls to go up on stage to sing a song. They'd been rehearsing it. It seemed a good idea. They were rather pretty and all in mini-skirts.'

'Yes?'

"Some of the boys started shouting 'Strip, strip, strip'. It was quite a joke to begin with. I was at the back of the hall and I couldn't help laughing, and didn't react immediately. Then it got serious, and the girls were retreating behind the curtains on the stage. And one of them threw a pair of panties out. Boys started to rush up to the stage, and I ran up to stop them and…" He paused, caught between laughing and an expression miming horror.

'But what happened to the thrown panties?' This, I confess, was a devilish diversion on my part.

He paused to think. 'There was such a melee I can't be sure. I think I made a boy who'd picked them up return them. I'd be surprised if the whole shambles didn't get back to the head, but I wasn't carpeted as it turned out. Fortunately I'd already given my notice in.'

These words coincided with our train's arrival at Upper

Holloway, something of which Jack was unaware until I told him. We ascended the steps from the platform to the Holloway Road.

It was now late in the evening, yet warm enough to be shirt-sleeved outside, and I was feeling uncomfortable in my suit. I walked down the Holloway Road, having parted from Jack, who looked sombre and preoccupied as I left him to wait for a bus. I turned into the street where I occupied alone a tiny second floor flat for what seemed the very reasonable sum of three pounds three shillings weekly. It was now quite dark.

On the far side of the road, the row of three-storey Victorian houses matching those on my side stretched out, tiny gardens and gates in front. There was a sudden commotion in one of these gardens, behind bushes: 'For God's sake, lay off me for five minutes,' a woman shouted. There was no-one else about in the street.

I called out: 'Is someone in trouble?' A man with a strong Irish accent rose up, a little unsteadily, behind the garden wall: 'Nobody here's in trouble,' he said. 'Are you in trouble?' Then a black man came out of a nearby house, and complained he couldn't sleep because of the noise.

I gave up my meagre consideration of humanitarian intervention, and opened the front door of the house where I and my landlady lived. She was a mostly unemployed middle aged actress – I can't get used to the term 'actor' for female players – whose main day to day concern was the welfare of her three cats, at least one of which was often missing. The house was without light when I entered. My landlady was either out or asleep.

A few minutes later I heard a female scream from the garden across the road, and this time I dialled 999 from my landlady's hall-based telephone. A few minutes later a police car and police motor cyclist arrived, but the couple had already gone. I had, apparently, got matters out of proportion. Soon the police also departed, and I went to bed.

Even now I can recall the dream I had that night. Jack O'Neill was galloping towards the stage of a school hall, a stage on which a pretty teenage girl had mischievously flung a pair of pink panties. Jack then stopped in his tracks, eyes wide, an aghast expression on his face, half-turned towards a doorway through which his wife Sally appeared on cue, arms folded, advancing and screaming at him: 'Explain this away if you can!' I had not yet met mad Sally, but in my dream she resembled the then Labour Secretary of State for Employment and Productivity, Barbara Castle, and, aping her, wore a bright red dress.

Then another figure appeared. It was Peter Dawlish, who, head shaking, uttered in a world-weary voice: 'Really, Jack, is this the image of yourself you wish to project to your students?' His bow tie, strangely, was growing a little face on each wing, twin faces, from each of which a mouth was drawling: 'I couldn't agree more.'

7

The next day, another warm and bright autumn occasion, I was back into the college. Once again, staff energies were to be expended on preparations for the term's real commencement: no students, no distractions. In fact signs of active preparations were slight or even invisible, though I may have been deceived by appearances. I found Jack O'Neill draped carelessly across an armchair in the staff room. This time a cheap and shiny brown belt circled the waist of his retirement-ready trousers, and as I addressed a 'hello' to him he was tucking a slim volume of the poetry of John Keats into a jacket pocket.

I recalled that the previous day Jack's wife had been planning to call on the Home Secretary to free herself from future police attention.

'How did your wife get on down in Westminster?' I asked.

'She's a resourceful woman,' he said, 'off-centre as she is. She got into the minister's private office with Thomas. She took things up with his private secretary. I think she gave him quite a talking to.'

'Any hands-off-from-police-persecution guarantees given as demanded by her?'

'No guarantees given. The only guarantee is that there's going to be an inquiry about how she managed to get in.'

He had spoken drily, not seeking to amuse. But continuing domestic anxieties did not prevent him from being alert to other developments around him. During the morning a full-time female student of bright and comely aspect – here

I borrow a description used by Jack on one occasion in my presence – called into the staff room, asking if her umbrella had been handed in. She'd left it, she said, in a particular classroom. No-one could help. But, just after she had left the room, Jack proceeded to suggest unhelpfully bawdy responses he could have made to her, including: 'Is it long, narrow and straight?' and 'It's in my trousers.'

He was in these moments bubbling with infectious merriment, but now he easily alighted on another subject, toning down the humour in his voice.

'You may have noticed I've abandoned the rope belt for a plastic one. A concession to respectability that I'm happy to make.'

'Have you always been a little chaotic, let us say, in some of your personal arrangements?' I enquired.

He responded gaily. "It certainly goes back to my school days. About a month before I took my school certificate, one of my teachers, a moneyed bachelor about town, took me out to a plush restaurant where he was well known. During the meal he said this – of course I can't remember the exact words – but it's near enough:

'O'Neill, in all my twenty years of teaching, I have never encountered such a disorderly human being. I have some specimens of your work in my bag. At first glance these look as if they had issued from the hand of a cretin. But on closer inspection, one can observe the evidence of a mind inspired.'"

I could not but be impressed.

The real, student-filled term began with a jolt. Over a few working days I was dementedly trying to stay abreast of my teaching commitments, preparing for the next day's work, or even for work two days ahead; planning to some extent what I would cover over the present term; getting to know the students' names and faces. All at once I was close to being engulfed by the task I had taken on. This was definitely more than I had bargained for.

At this stage I had only a misty sense of the personalities of some of my colleagues, but I was getting acquainted now with one person outside the English studies sector. This was Bob Hardy, who headed the little knot of teachers assigned to the subject of government, local and otherwise. He was indisputably a lively figure. Above the middle height, he had regular features, and a high forehead. I guessed he was in his late twenties.

His manner was open, chatty, matey. His unofficial and self-given functions, like those of Stanley Payne, included identifying personal flaws in other staff members, but Bob was especially fixated on those in management positions who had attracted his irritation or wrath. I had exchanged greetings with him a couple of times in the annexe's corridors, had seen him talking with people in the staff room, and I had introduced myself to him as a new legal apparatchik. He had a restless air, even teeth and – when not provoked, which he frequently was – had a wide and generous grin.

One day in mid-September, on Bob's suggestion, I joined him for a special price five shillings apiece lunch, with a narrow range of options, in a Chinese restaurant a few doors along from the Denmark Arms. I asked him, before the chicken and sweetcorn soup arrived, how he got on with the head of department and his deputy.

Bob did not mince his words: 'Pringle is no problem. Oliver Price calls him a gentleman. I'd call him a benign nonentity. Fawcett is a little shit capable of being a big shit. He's a tale carrier, a rumour monger, a shit stirrer, a nose picker and a fag roasting prefect at heart. He also likes to pretend he's one of the boys. Fortunately he's trying hard to get promotion somewhere else. He's nasty enough to succeed.' He paused for a few seconds, looking at me directly, and humorously: 'You have probably gathered I'm not wholeheartedly a fan of his.'

'Have you had run-ins with him then?'

'Not half. I know he reported me for being late into classes. Pringle asked to see me about it.'

'And?'

'I said to Pringle his information was wrong. I said his spies were unreliable and he should get himself better spies. I think he believed me. I don't think it was exactly the reaction he was expecting. Then I went to see David Fawcett. I said a little birdie told me that he'd told Pringle I was turning up late for classes.'

I looked at him. Confronting the people in charge so directly hadn't occurred to me as a wise or optional tactic. He went on.

'He didn't deny it. I told him that if he reached such a conclusion again, I'd be obliged if he'd discuss it with me first, so that I could put him right if his conclusion was misconceived.'

'His reply?'

'He was quiet. He's better at dealing with weak responses.'

By this time the soup had arrived for both of us and there was an interval before discussion re-started.

'There was another occasion too,' Bob resumed.

'What was that about?'

'Did you know that when not actually teaching, outside class-contact time, we're supposed to be on departmental duty?'

'You mean we're expected to stay in the building?'

'That's the idea. It's inherited from the past.'

'Local customary law,' I contributed cleverly, before returning to my soup.

"Anyway, during a break between lectures, I went over to the Co-op to do some shopping. I ran into Fawcett coming out. He said: 'You should be on departmental, Bob, during non-teaching hours.'"

"'It's OK,' I said. 'I'm not on departmental. This errand is strictly during teaching time. My class is waiting for me with considerable impatience.' I went straight past him into the shop. Of course it wasn't teaching time."

'Might you be riding for a fall?'

'Maybe I am.'

Our main courses had arrived – noodles for Bob, sweet and sour pork for me, and we tucked in. I asked, when clear speech was possible:

'You've not needed to involve our union rep to date? Shirley Tait, I believe?'

For a moment I thought he was embarrassed. Then he said quietly: 'I can fight my own wars.'

'What do you think of that chap with the bow tie, English studies?' I asked.

Bob was short. 'Peter Dawlish. You've probably summed him up yourself. I don't get on too well with him. But he's not a sneak and not always a prefect.'

'What's the problem with him, do you think?'

'Surely you've noticed he's a self-important snob? But that's just his personality, so I suppose we shouldn't complain.' Bob ate a mouthful. Then he said, reflectively:

'Do you know, when he first came, I was so startled by his bow tie and noblesse oblige and what not, that when he put out a hand I was too stunned to shake it. It's typical of him, you know, that when he travels by train, he always goes first class.'

'First class?'

'First class.'

He went on: 'Last term there was quite a funny moment involving Peter. I was in the annexe staff room. One of the liberal studies teachers, in fact Shirley, had taken a group of students out to a church dating back to medieval times, and had done brass rubbings.'

I was surprised. This was one of my impromptu learning days. 'Brass rubbings – part of liberal studies?'

'Certainly,' said Bob. "You can do that in liberal studies. It's a big country. You can show films. Then the civic awareness course has a section called 'Boys and Girls'. The list of topics covered includes venereal disease and homosexuality. They are the last two in the list. No kidding. Tape recorded talks. But brass rubbings make an occasional diversion."

'So where did Peter Dawlish come into this?'

"Well, one of these rubbings was laid out on the staff room table, and Peter came in, sticking his pipe into his mouth and taking it out again. He looked over the rubbing and read the words inscribed on it. 'Medieval Latin', he said, and translated it. It was something like 'Our Lord who looks after us'. I couldn't resist having a bit of fun.

So I said 'Naaow... that's pre-medieval.' Peter got a bit impatient. He got up, went over to his briefcase, got a book out and started flicking through the pages, pulling at his pipe and sucking a bit more. Then he said: 'I know medieval Latin when I see it. I did it for my Schools.'"

'And then?'

"'Naaow,' I said again. 'That's pre-medieval all right. You can tell by the design.'

He stomped off out of the room muttering something about red brick universities."

I laughed out loud at all this. The little remaining of my sweet and sour pork and fried rice looked unappetising now, but I launched a final attack on it before contributing:

'But Bow Tie's present post of assistant lecturer in English in this low level tech college can't sit well with his perception of his superior role in the world.'

'He's trying hard to get out of it,' said Bob. 'English lecturers in further education are six a farthing, and it may take him a while. He puts in job applications on the quiet. And he's not the only one.'

'Who else then?'

'Most of us.' Bob adopted a half-serious, half-comic tone. 'This place is a bit like a German prisoner-of-war camp in the films. Escape plans are being constantly hatched. They have to be solo efforts, of course. No mass break-outs, and you don't get shot if you're caught. But once you're under the wire and outside, the problem is you find you're in another camp like this one. You might have more money, more seniority, more privileges. But you're still a prisoner. A lot of us don't get that far. We dig tunnels, but are foiled each time. Then we sulk and after a while make plans again. And when we fail our morale goes into a decline.'

'I take it you're applying for jobs then,' I put in perceptively.

'All the time,' said Bob. The meal finished, we paid our separate bills.

All this left me with cause for reflection. One thing was clear. Some of my new colleagues at East Ham had problems or were unsettled. And might Bob Hardy, if no-one else, be destined for the sack at some point? Being soft-hearted, I began to be concerned about his future, as well as about that of Jack O'Neill and little Thomas. And I wondered about the mental health of my colleague-in-law, Ann Feldman. Soon after, the weekend arrived.

8

On the Saturday evening I had arranged to meet a friend from recent Nottingham University days. This was Alan, who like me had studied law, but unlike me was already in his later twenties. Law was his second degree, as he had previously collected one in sociology. A county grant had supported him through the first process; a paternal grant had enabled him to cruise through the second, and between these two courses he had given a year to voluntary service overseas He was now enrolled on a master's degree course, also father-supported, in international law at London's University College. His student life seemed set to continue indefinitely.

We met up at the Gilbert and Sullivan public house, just off the Strand and not far from Charing Cross. I had previously decided, after finding the place by chance, that I liked (besides the availability of standard beer options), the circularity of the large room, and the G & S-related pictures on the walls and pillars.

Alan was theoretically a socialist, and actually one, in his own view. I wasn't politically active myself, or even a committed armchair adherent to a precise political creed, but some of my friends at University had been more definite. They often seemed to have livelier minds and to live livelier lives than the others. I was merely on the social fringe of the Campaign for Nuclear Disarmament and of the socialist groups, while resolutely declining membership of anything and handing out leaflets, though I did go on an occasional march as a limited concession. I escaped, whenever possible, partisan political arguments in the student union bar. I do not know why my socialist friends put up with me, unless it was because they imagined that one day I might find routine commitment to political action irresistible.

Alan was mostly in the margins of activity, so far as I could see. He was more of a party-goer than a party member, but he did, by all accounts, go on demonstrations and attend political meetings quite often. He also read books, though perhaps not as many as he implied, some of them certainly of interest to left-wingers, and he was generally voluble about the world's conflicts.

Anyway, while awaiting him I sat for a short time nursing a pint of draught bitter in the G & S, which was less than half full in the early evening, taking in the associated light opera memorabilia pictures around me. It was not a noisy pub. No recorded music, not even Gilbert and Sullivan numbers. One framed musical item, close to me on a pillar, was the front page of a long ago programme for the opera *HM Pinafore*, and next to it was the sheet music of its notoriously patriotic song – *For he is an Englishman*. After inspecting these, I gathered up fragments of conversations at other tables, and noticed at the bar, waiting to be served, a slim and intense-looking girl with a mass of dark hair.

Alan swept in, animated as usual, and, as he reached my table, spotted the 'Englishman' music, denigrating it promptly as trash belonging to dead times of empire. I went up to the bar, standing next to the slim girl, and bought him a pint, while he lounged at our table. While I was at the bar, the girl, now served, picked up two glasses carefully, and before moving, looked across the room in Alan's direction. He was quite tall, with a fresh open face, and a mop of dark curly hair. He hailed from the north, Wigan or somewhere near it. Confidence and decisiveness streamed out of him. I don't suppose he was especially good looking, but he was responsive to what was happening around him and had presence. I had little doubt he had spotted the girl looking at him. She had joined another girl, shorter, less slim, laughing, loud, at a table close to ours.

Alan was first into talk with me, lofting questions about what I was doing, and I gave him a light-hearted run down of that, not leaving out the wine-coloured corduroy jacket of Peter Dawlish, or the troubles of Jack O'Neill and the latter's insane wife.

The slim girl and her companion were just within Alan's field of vision. As we sat, I caught a phrase or two of the conversation between the two girls and the single word 'Nottingham'. Alan turned towards them and smiled at them before turning back.

I asked about Alan's girlfriend, who'd been around for years, living apart from him but nevertheless an attachment of a kind. 'She's fine,' he said, impatiently. I didn't enquire if he had other amours running. He often did, or so I heard from others.

The conversation moved on. Alan was now well started on his higher degree, he told me, while working part time to finance himself. He said that parental grants for him were largely time-expired, and that the parental wish was that he find himself a proper job. He wondered if a few hours a week of law teaching at my college might come his way.

I expressed doubts. Then at that moment, without ceremony he turned his head and chipped into the conversation of the two girls nearby.

'Did you say something about Nottingham? I've just come down from there.' The answer that came back promptly was from the shorter girl, and was that he had better go back there then, but it was true that Nottingham had been mentioned for some reason, and they were not discouraging in their looks.

'Can we join you?' asked Alan, already rising from our table.

Within a few seconds we were with them, and the conversation, once begun, did not stop until the girls left a while later. Before they did so, we had learned their names and even more about them. Martine was the slim, intense-looking one, and Marion was the shorter and noisier.

9

Next morning, Sunday, I woke up in my hidey-hole off the Holloway Road, and without company, when it was still quite dark. The old terraced house was silent, and I was conscious of the stillness of the street, save for measured lashing of rain against the drop-stained window. I looked out. On every hand I could see dripping from gutters and glistening surfaces, and there were puddles galore on the uneven pavement below. The rain was steady, persistent, and there was the impression nothing of this had altered for a very long time. No lights were on in neighbouring houses, and no-one was walking in the street. The external world seemed depressed and defeated, while I felt unjustifiably upbeat.

I allowed myself to doze off again. When I woke it was light and the radio, when switched on, was immediately ready with news. Flooding in many places was reported, and later that day Clapham Junction was said to be under water, the Portsmouth Road impassable, and Southend cut off. The paper boy had braved the rain to deliver a soggy Sunday paper – mine, not my landlady's – but its headlines and news stories did not add to the day's grounds for good cheer. The Vietnam war, which I was to learn, long after its conclusion, was called by the Vietnamese 'the American war', seemed set for indefinite duration. Richard Nixon was being talked up as the next US President, while in Britain the Conservative politician Enoch Powell, who had made a notorious speech earlier in the year, passing on, in dramatic terms, the fears and anger of some white people about the impact on their lives of immigration by black people, was being touted as a probable presence in the Conservative government in Britain, once the present Harold-Wilson-led Labour government had fallen from power.

There were forebodings that an intensification of international tensions, consequent upon the stomping on democratic reforms in Czechoslovakia a few weeks before by Soviet armed forces, was an inevitable development. In my hidey-hole, now less upbeat, I felt insulated to a degree from the wider world's problems and awfulness; was able to hide from these and the rain for the moment. I escaped into a novel I had begun to read days before. It was the first volume in Anthony Powell's *Music of Time* sequence, presenting a luxuriously descriptive tale, set in the nineteen twenties, of schoolboy life at an ancient public school: in which snobbery, aspiration, social awkwardness and practical joke revenge for a housemaster's fussiness, occupy much space. As I entered the book's inner chambers, I began to feel still less oppressed by the harsher and nastier world in which I actually lived, while acquiring more admiration for Powell's narrative talent than for his elite world characters.

Some of that day I spent reading and loafing more, fitting in a duty phone call to my Sussex-based parents and, when the rain faltered, a walk down the Holloway Road and on to Islington's Angel road junction (coaching inn long gone) and back. I arrived back at the front door at the same time as one of the cats. Entering the hall I confronted my landlady, who greeted her cat's return with fondness and mine more mechanically. I could not complain. I imagined that my landlady, fiftyish, small, slight, wearing no make-up and having a dried-up appearance, gained much relief from loneliness from her feline children.

Later that day I wrote out a plan for the week's work ahead, and even reached beyond that by making notes for a couple of 'lectures' which were really lessons.

10

The next day, Monday, drizzling rain accompanied me persistently on my journey to the college, requiring much umbrella use whenever I was not under other cover. That day also produced other developments. The first of these happened in the café where I had first met Jack O'Neill, and which was also often visited, I had been told, by Oliver Price and Peter Dawlish.

The place was mostly empty of customers, and not one of these three colleagues was present. But the fourth member of the English studies group, Shirley Tait, whom I so far knew only by sight, was, as I entered, about to move away from the counter with a cup of tea, exchanging friendly words with the man behind the counter. Shirley was slight of stature, not quite petite but on the way there, had plentiful fair hair, full lips, a snub nose and large eyes. More than that, she radiated a warm personality.

Having acquired my own tea, I approached her table, first telling her, so to speak, my name and rank.

'Yes, of course,' she said.

'Do you mind if I join you?'

'Not at all. What a foul day.'

I agreed and said something about having met Jack O'Neill for the first time in the café on my first day at the college. Her eyes, which were blue, perhaps bluer even than Jack O'Neill's, I speculated, and certainly sufficient in themselves for him to dream about, lit up. 'He is quite something, isn't he?' she said.

'I gather that you take students to do brass rubbings,' I said, changing the subject.

'Not one of the most magical activities,' she said, 'but it's on the recommended list.'

'And why did you become trade union rep?' I queried.

'Your conversation does dart about,' she said. 'You're a lawyer, I know. Do you do that in cross-examination?'

I laughed. 'Touché.' Shirley was already displaying, I decided, as astute a mind as any I had so far seen functioning at the college.

'You're evading my question,' I asserted. 'I don't know anything about union reps.'

'Well,' she said. 'I think staff need support when picked on by management. But only one other Department in the college – Engineering – has one. Sometimes it's not much more than being a witness at meetings. Sometimes there's much more involvement than that. Even senior lecturers can be vulnerable.'

'Mr. Pringle doesn't give the impression of being a tyrant,' I observed.

'Far from it,' she conceded.

'Bob Hardy was telling me that he's had a bust-up or two with David Fawcett.'

Shirley looked at me calmly, wondering, I suspected, if I was trying to pump her for information about Bob.

'He doesn't need me to rescue him, and that's a fact.' She turned the conversation in my direction. 'There are two of you, aren't there, teaching law? You and Ann.'

I agreed. 'You've joined the college lecturers' union?' was her next question.

I confirmed that I had put the membership form in the branch treasurer's pigeon-hole. 'I don't know about Ann,' I added.

'She told me she's not interested. Unfortunately, she may

need the union's help....' Her words tailed off before she added: 'as any of us might do some time.'

Both interested in the subject and attracted to Shirley, I plunged in gauchely, changing the topic again. 'I must go to the staff room now, but it would be great to talk more about union activities. Perhaps I could have a drink with you after work one evening.'

She said nothing for a few moments – whether many of her colleagues wanted to talk with her about union matters I doubted – but did not seem disconcerted by the suggestion. 'That would be nice,' she said politely. She said no more but I sensed with sorrow it was too early in our acquaintance to attempt to pin her down with a proposal for a diaried assignation. My friend Alan, I knew, would not have been as cautious.

That day I was in college and moving between classrooms and the little home base room containing my very own desk. My law teaching colleague, Ann, was also about somewhere. I wasn't present when she appeared, but I learnt later from Stanley Payne in Ann's absence that she had arrived with 'her new man', said to be Canadian and working on a newspaper.

Peter Dawlish's reported comment in the staff room about Ann's new man and Bob Hardy's rebuke in response were to be repeated more than once by listeners that day. 'I'll swear there's more than Canadian blood in him,' the former had said, while Bob had thrown back: 'I suppose that's your strange way of saying that he's Jewish.'

The purpose of Ann's bringing in her husband's replacement seemed to be to show him where she worked, without introducing him to any of her colleagues. Introductions there were none.

Stanley told me that he had at first assumed the man was Ann's estranged husband. Ann had seen the Canadian off the premises without haste, and had then joined her class, for which she was late, her students having advanced close to mutiny while waiting for her. Stanley reported that Ann had told him at some point that her parents were happier about the new man because he was Jewish, and her husband was not. This confirmed that Ann herself was Jewish, when her surname had for me only raised that possibility.

Stanley went on, telling me of 'an Ann mystery'. 'There's a letter in Ann's tray that came on Friday, which she won't open. And a telegram arrived for her today and she won't open that either. I don't know what that's all about.'

Stanley was a man, I felt, who was not one to exhibit frantic curiosity, but I could see he would welcome an explanation.

When I finally reached the little staff room that morning, both Ann and her pervasive perfume were present. She looked lost in thought. Stanley Payne had told me that Ann had the look of a real sexual vulture, but that may have said more about him than about her. It seemed to me that the real person behind her enticing exterior appearance was signalled by her inward looking preoccupation with disaster and by her social passivity. She seemed to me more prey than predator. I greeted Ann in a friendly fashion and asked how she was. In her low, unmusical voice, she said she was all right, but in a dilemma.

'I think I told you,' she said, 'my husband left me.'

'At Christmas, if I remember.'

'Yes. He went off with someone else. But now he's changed his mind. He wants me back. He's ringing all the time and sending me letters and telegrams. And there's this other person I've been with. And he wants to marry me too. I was going to, once I got divorced that is, until my ex started contacting me again. I'm worried about him. He's been off work and he's been in a state about it.'

This was, I considered, though not spoken quickly, or with intense emotion, an anguished unburdening. I was at a loss.

It was not a situation I had come across in my life or anyone else's.

'That's a dilemma,' I agreed. I went on, inanely: 'Some people would think they are fortunate to be in that situation. A choice between two, then.' I should have been more sympathetic, but felt out of my depth, so had tried flippancy with a solemn air. Even now I can be cross with myself for things I said so long ago.

'I don't know what to do,' she said. 'I'd like to go away and think. The trouble is, this job's getting in the way.'

Unqualified to advise, I thanked her for telling me, and hoped it would get sorted out. Ann's prognosis that a meteor would soon arrive to destroy the world seemed to have been ushered into the background. I escaped to a class of trainee cost and works accountants, who were expected to learn something about commercial law from me. For the next hour I did my best to meet their learning needs.

On my return to the little room, Ann had gone, but a bouquet of flowers, all without exception chrysanthemums, wrapped in neat cellophane, had been delivered and was resting on her desk. Her phantom husband, I concluded, had struck again.

That day there seemed to be little relief from the difficulties of others around me. Jack O'Neill had appeared, late and unshaven. He had been caught up with getting his wife into hospital again, and their little son Thomas was with him in college. In the afternoon Jack had teaching to do. I said I could look after Thomas for him. My offer was accepted gratefully, even with surprise. 'I am rescued.'

This was a novel duty for me. I found myself alone with this three-year-old in the large staff room. He babbled a lot, identified items he could see through the window, poured imaginary cups of tea, played a ring a ring o' roses game with me, and drew pictures with me too. At one moment three female students, looking for his father, appeared at the staff room door. When I told them Thomas was Mr. O'Neill's son, they took an admiring interest in him. Thomas took one look at them, hid behind me, and loudly and firmly said 'No'. I deduced that he felt safer with men. Before his father reappeared he had to my consternation – I use Jack's later words – empowered his bowels to fill his underpants. It was a situation I was unable to address. When Jack did arrive, and I told him of this troubling development, he immediately reached for a reel of paper napkins in his briefcase.

'Better to use these than essay papers, whether marked or unmarked,' he remarked breezily.

I returned with relief to my desk, and noticed that the chrysanthemums for Ann were now standing in a waterless milk bottle.

Before long, college duties were over and I was sharing a tube train to Barking and then the overland train to Upper Holloway with Jack O'Neill and little Thomas. The rain had come to a halt at last. During our journey Jack referred to one of the three girls who had looked at Thomas with adoration as Mary, whom he confirmed was the girl who had recently enquired after her missing umbrella. 'She sets every reptilian nerve a-quiver,' he confessed. 'She writes artlessly and beautifully,' he added, 'uncorrupted by education, rather like Shelagh Delaney, yet there's also something quite worldly about her.'

'Did she locate her umbrella somewhere other than in your trousers,' I asked. 'I'd like to think so.'

He ignored my attempt at humour. 'She's the only student I address by her Christian name,' he said. 'I probably shouldn't address her in such a caressing manner in class,' he continued. "They were struggling to understand this Wilfred Owen poem where a girl gives a rose to a soldier. I said to Mary: 'What would be my position if you gave me a rose?' She replied, rising to the occasion: 'Well, you'd be doing all right, wouldn't you?' This drew applause from her classmates. I said: 'Well, I would certainly cancel all my appointments.'" As Jack came out with this, I observed that he pronounced every syllable distinctly. The class had, he added, dissolved into anarchic mirth for the umpteenth time in the session. The first time, he said, had been right at the beginning.

'So what produced the first explosion?' He was more than ready to tell me.

"I'm completely hopeless about females. I couldn't find the class in the first place. I was wandering from room to room, looking for it. I couldn't remember what course it was, or who I was looking for. Then I found the class, and Mary was sitting in the front row. I said to them: 'Ah, some girls' faces I remember. Now I know I'm in the right room. That's how I find my way around the world. Everything else is just a blur.' After that, there was a good deal of disorder, and time passed before I could make myself heard again."

I was, frankly, envious of the amazing vitality of his eloquence and sense of fun about himself and the world. 'Will your students, do you think, get good exam results?'

'Who knows? But will any of them be able to say they have not been kept stimulated and happy?'

I saw him become pre-occupied again, obviously troubled about something. 'I don't know what I'm going to do about arrangements for looking after Thomas on Wednesday and Thursday evenings, when I'm teaching. I daren't ask the people who are looking after him during the day at the moment.' Thomas during the journey had been nursing a soft toy – a cloth rabbit – and had hardly looked up at his father.

Jack hadn't been angling for me to volunteer child care, but I offered my services. Soon after, we were out of the train, and then Jack and Thomas were waiting for a bus to take them to Crouch End. There Jack and Sally had recently purchased, on a mortgage, a ground floor flat. Leaving them, I walked the short distance to my own home, and made myself something to eat. I was still very much enjoying having my own place of retreat. Sharing flats was for the past.

I had had a 'steady' relationship with a girl during my last university year and even earlier, but this had become 'unsteady'. She had with increasing dedication become wedded to a serious academic career, spending more and more time researching, researching, while I had continued to be wedded more to life outside work, and my removal to London had added to, and underlined, the growing divergence between us. So the relationship had died, and we had become at best distant friends.

I must make a small admission here. The truth is that when with Alan in the Gilbert and Sullivan, I had obtained the phone number of the flat rented by Martine and Marion, and had in mind inviting out Marion, the shorter and louder of the pair. I had not got round to it yet in the whirl of first engagement with teaching, and perhaps too because my interest in her was ambivalent. If I telephoned her, would she remember me? I could at least test the waters. I knew of no other woman at that moment to whom I might make an approach.

11

Next day, Tuesday, the weather was brighter, but cooler. I had woken dangerously late, and reached the little station with a full briefcase, only to find trains eastward had been delayed. I descended to the platform with anxious frustration growing inside me. Glancing back at the steps up to the ticket office, I noticed two men coming down, one behind the other. The hindmost was a railwayman, a slim, small, dark skinned man with a moustache, perhaps born in Britain, perhaps not many years before living somewhere in the Indian sub-continent. He was walking quickly, close on the heels of a big man in his twenties, a white working class Londoner. As a train unexpectedly pulled in, reducing my fear of lateness, I heard the railwayman ask the big man repeatedly – I imagined there were obvious grounds for asking the question – if he'd got a ticket. In those days electronic entry controls were not present to decide the question.

'No I haven't. Talk properly, can't you?' was the answer. 'You're showing me up in front of all these people, you ignorant pig.' The railwayman walked away without uttering a reply. I entered a carriage, having seen the big white man striding away and then stepping into the next one. Observed racist incident closed.

Making it to college just as metaphorical clocks struck nine, I raced into my first teaching session. There was no time to think until the mid-morning break. Arriving then in the niche room where I had my desk, I noted that Ann's milk-bottled but waterless chrysanthemums were all present and correct, but on a slow but undeniable progress towards dissolution. Ann was also present, and was quietly absorbed in correcting, or at least marking, essays.

In the annexe staff room to which I resorted next, talk of plans for change in the college was afoot. Peter Dawlish said he'd heard our antiquated annexe was to be pulled down and used for non-educational purposes. The main building, he had been told, was to become an administrative educational block, and we'd be redeployed elsewhere. In his resonant voice, devoid of any trace of a Welsh accent, Oliver Price produced a different, but perhaps connected, rumour: that we were to be incorporated into the new Polytechnic planned for the area.

There was mention too, of the role of the Chief Education Officer, a powerful eminence grise of a man, hovering in the Town Hall shadows, said to be seen occasionally in the main building, and to be making life and death decisions over the head of the reportedly malleable Principal Plummer. This man from the council was to be feared, I gathered, for crude cash-saving decisions more than to be revered for dedication to the cause of education. Yet nobody I spoke to seemed to have met him.

Several fellow staff members, standing in a group, were united in exasperation over a short memorandum from head of department Mr. Pringle. This had been pinned up on the staff notice board. It informed us that staff and students henceforth should not use the short cut through the Town Hall when transferring from the multi-storey main building over the road to and from the annexe. There were irritated expressions of defiance. Bob Hardy said, without heat, that he was going to ignore it. It was ridiculous to have to go the long way round. Peter Dawlish said portentously:

'It's vital that staff are allowed to pass freely through the Town Hall corridor. Otherwise how can we possibly discourage students from trespassing there?'

I settled into a corner where two liberal studies teachers, Martin, a man in early middle age, with a German accent and a thick brush of jet black hair, and Shirley Tait, were already seated. I have not said much about the liberal studies teachers as yet. There were half a dozen or more of them altogether, headed by a senior lecturer called Dai Griffiths, who had taken up his post the previous term and had already attracted, seemingly with justification, considerable unpopularity amongst the staff he led. Shirley was listening to Martin, occasionally pushing back out of the way her abundant fair hair.

Martin, using language carefully, was in the process of pulling Dai Griffiths, who was not during this discussion in the room, to pieces. Unlike Oliver Price, Griffiths had a voice which immediately celebrated his Welsh origin. Argumentative by nature, his physical appearance resembled that of public school hero Billy Bunter, if his jutting out teeth and significant hair loss were left out of account. Martin spoke about him in scathing terms. 'He does practically no work: if the subject titles look neat and plausible he doesn't care a damn what happens in practice,' he said, speaking slowly and with great deliberation.

Shirley agreed and suggested their senior lecturer was all set to become a head of department. Then she said she'd been told off by him for being – most unusually for her – half an hour late one morning, and had been compared unfavourably with a colleague Herbert, whose record for time-keeping was said to set an example for everyone else. She had given as good as she had received in reply, saying blithely that half an hour of herself was worth an hour of Herbert any day. This, I gathered, had not been an acceptable response. She emphasised that she hated being late for anything and rarely was.

'Herbert seems to me a nice man,' I threw in, interrupting their flow. Though I haven't previously mentioned Herbert,

I had spent half an hour or more in his pleasant, candid and unassuming elder statesman company. He spoke to everyone as an equal, with the assistance of an easy public school voice and manner, and a kindly naiveté.

He was in his mid or late fifties, said to have retired from business because of a heart attack or a nervous breakdown. No-one seemed to know for certain which it was, though Bob Hardy had told me that Herbert bore all the signs of having suffered both conditions, probably repeatedly, to judge from his appearance and activity-level. I never saw Herbert looking well, though his natural cheerfulness shone through. He seemed to have spent his whole life being exceptionally and amiably conformist. Yet he had confided to me, a few days previously, that his liberal studies students seemed most incurious. They didn't seem to want to know anything outside what was necessary to occupy their place in life.

He proceeded to illustrate this point. He told me that when he had been about nineteen, he had been a junior clerk in a firm which had a factory in Birmingham. He had 'some audacity at that age'. Having planned a cycling holiday in Belgium, he'd asked his boss if it could be arranged that he look over the sister factory in that country. The boss had been astonished at the request. But Herbert had only asked out of interest, and when he had visited the factory in Belgium, he had a marvellous time. They had shown him all over, given him lunch…

'Of course all that was well before the war,' he had ended, as if the world had then been simpler and sunnier.

The conversation between Martin, Shirley, and to a lesser extent, myself, was continuing. Shirley was saying: 'Herbert's a sweetie, but he hasn't got a clue. Teaching liberal studies you have to be radical, unconventional or you're a waste of time. Herbert, lovely as he is, is totally without value as a liberal studies teacher. He'd make a nice chairman, I'm sure, of a gentlemen's club,' she conceded.

'Not of our Association of Teachers in Technical Institutions' union branch?' I threw out lightly.

'I think not.' Shirley then looked at me and said: 'You did say you'd joined the union, didn't you, Clive?' I confirmed this, and Martin smiled benevolently at her: 'You rightly remind us, Shirley, that we should not be pushovers.'

'I don't think you're wanting in that respect, Martin.'

Pressing back with one hand his brush of dark hair, which was not at all susceptible to efforts to do so, Martin changed topic. He looked over at me, and said in his earnest and deliberate fashion: 'Do you know we have been enjoined to provide end of term marks for liberal studies students? Our führer, Dai Griffiths, insists on it. The question is – what do we give marks for?'

'Well, what for?' I enquired patiently. (I must admit freely here, that if some of the sense of Martin's exposition remains intransigently in my memory, the detail of it was captured rather more completely in my journal.)

'We have constructive ideas for this.' Martin's German accent seemed even more pronounced than earlier, while his speech was proceeding at the same snail-like speed. 'Students taking liberal studies as part of their academic commitment should be marked out of ten. A student should start with one mark for looking awake; one more for actually being awake; one for appearing to be interested; one for asking a question; another if the question is sensible; another if the question is not only sensible but reveals intelligence. That's six, and if you get six, you can turn that into 60%. Mind you, if you score that high, it is arguable that you do not need the benefit of liberal studies.' Martin completed this exposition by grinning broadly for some seconds. He had certainly produced comedy, if comedy of an elephantine kind.

'So what do you teach in liberal studies?' I asked both of them.

'Well,' said Martin. 'Various things. Our führer Mr. Dai Griffiths has devised a collection of titles this year. We're following them, but some of us have been questioning the validity of these titles.'

Martin's delivery was so ponderous, for me like the slow ticking of a large and ancient clock, that to interrupt his exposition was tempting, but I listened attentively.

"Four titles are 'Civic Awareness', 'Economic Awareness', 'Communications' and 'Aesthetic Appreciation'. I told our führer that there should be no boundaries between subjects. The idea of liberal studies is that discussion should be free."

'Sounds reasonable to me.'

'Unfortunately he did not begin to understand what I was talking about, or that I was taking a rise out of him.'

Martin continued. "I asked him: 'Where do you draw the line between 'Economic Awareness' and 'Civic Awareness'. I pointed out that in both, from the moment you open your mouth, you are teaching 'Communications'." Martin now produced a smile.

'So what did your führer have to say to that?'

'Oh,' he said: 'It's just one of those unfortunate overlaps.'

Martin completed his brick by brick verbal demolition of the senior lecturer in liberal studies with sweeping scorn. 'He gets away with eight hours' teaching time weekly and he's planning to reduce that if he can get away with it. He's such an opportunist that he finds it difficult to believe anyone else might not be an opportunist.'

'He's lazy, self-seeking and generally unpleasant,' adjudged Shirley, who seemed to have inside knowledge of Griffiths, but who spoke without rancour in her voice.

'He's Welsh too,' I said foolishly.

'I'll ignore that,' said Shirley, with a glimmer of a smile, as if she wasn't necessarily attributing zenophobia to me. 'I just don't support lazy opportunist rule for liberal studies in this godforsaken dump. But since he's applying for head of department jobs, he shouldn't be with us long. When he goes, we'll have had four liberal studies chiefs in the three years I've been here.'

There was much character in Shirley's face, and I was entranced as before both by her looks and by her lucid, calm and forceful way of putting things. 'I'm beginning to think,' I said, 'that this isn't quite the harmonious place I thought it would be.'

'Wait till you see the blood and the bodies,' said Shirley shortly, but with another smile.

I wondered at that moment what opinion Stanley Payne had of her. I had heard nothing either complimentary or condemnatory so far.

Later that morning I walked over to the canteen for lunch with Peter Dawlish. Looking through a window, before we sat down Dawlish identified two students' cars parked in what was considered officially to be the 'staff car park'. He was in the habit of stationing his own two-seater sports car there, and in consequence had a proprietary interest. 'Cheeky buggers,' he said. 'I'll take that up with the caretaker.'

12

I was by now developing some familiarity with the conversation culture of the staff room.

This must have varied from that, say, of the engineering department, and of course it reflected the sort of people who had come to teach English, liberal studies and the business studies range. That Tuesday afternoon, at the break, I was exposed to some attitudes about race and colour. After some talk about the looming American Presidential election, the name of Conservative politician Enoch Powell, who had, predicting race war in Britain, made his 'Rivers of Blood' speech in Birmingham the previous April, came up. Oliver Price suggested that Powell should not be condemned merely for articulating what 'many people' had been thinking.

I looked at Oliver, whom I had come to identify as a loyal occupant of the 'sensible' political ground. Within the broad confines of his face, his ample cheeks, as well as his narrow eyes, were not close to each other. His demeanour was not aggressive to the slightest degree. He was the reasonable man in the street. His assumptions about the world around him were now put under pressure.

"In 'many people' you include white Anglo-Saxons intermarried with Norman conquest invaders and their descendants, and then intermarried maybe with incoming refugees such as Huguenots?" asked Bob Hardy lightly.

'All right, granted,' said Oliver Price.

'Jewish people from wherever too?'

'Of course.' Bob Hardy stepped up his attack.

'So you wouldn't have joined in with Powell types early this century who went in for appalling anti-Semitism against Jews taking sanctuary here from pogroms in Ukraine?'

'They were Powell types, were they?' (Price put his query sceptically, but mildly.)

'And you would have stood up bravely against our Prime Ministers of the Thirties – more Powell types – who were friendly with Hitler despite his outrageous persecution of Jews in Germany?'

Price was silent at this point. Bob Hardy followed up what he took to be a small advantage gained. 'What Powell should be condemned for is sanitising ignorant and gross attitudes by whites of their superiority over coloured people. That's despicable.'

'And isn't that,' I chimed in innocently but in a neutral, almost puzzled, tone, to the observable surprise of Oliver Price, who had, perhaps, marked me down as destined to listen and learn more than talk, 'more or less the same as articulating what many people had been thinking?'

Price's surprise was replaced by a frown which soon faded.

'Despicable thinking,' said Jack O'Neill, magisterial for a moment, 'is deeply rooted in many white people, often deep down where we don't want to admit it, and not very deep down in the case of my wife.'

There was a short silence, and shop talk of a sort then replaced it. Oliver Price showed no obvious sign of either shame or defensiveness. But instead of sticking with the subject of racism, he adopted, swiftly and diplomatically, the strategy of shifting to less angry subject-matter, and spoke of the importance of personal appearance at teaching post interviews, as if this was as worthy and weighty a conversational subject as racism, and one which could succeed it with natural ease.

'Maybe it's obvious,' he explained, 'but the ideal appearance at an interview is not to have just had a haircut, but to have had one a week ago, not to shine your shoes specially, but always to have shiny shoes.'

'But what about the person on the other side of the interviewing table? What about the interviewer's outfit?' I challenged, adding, with as genuine a face as I could put together:

'Should he' – for I had not then heard of female interviewers – 'be smartly and conventionally turned out too? Isn't there an argument for the opposite? If the person doing the interviewing wears jeans, old open-toed sandals, a Hawaian shirt and hasn't had a haircut or a beard-trim for a year or two, he could assess candidates' reactions to the contrast in turn-out between them and himself as well as candidates' responses to the questions. It could be quickly spotted whether the interviewee is at a loss or not. An easily shocked would-be teacher is obviously in the wrong line of work. The jaw-droppers could be filtered out of the short-list.'

As I came out with this subversive blather, Price was watching me carefully, and gave no clue that he had registered that what I had said bordered on the humorous. 'I don't think that's contributing usefully to the discussion,' he said. 'Are you an iconoclast?'

Jack O'Neill's interjection saved me from answering. 'I made an effort to be well turned out at my interview here.'

Said Peter Dawlish: 'But you were scruffy.'

'It's all relative, of course,' said Oliver Price.

Jack added: 'But at least I didn't go down badly for other reasons. When I started applying for teaching jobs a few years ago, they asked me at my first interview why I had applied. I said it had been years since I'd gone in for this interview lark. It probably wasn't the right thing to say.'

'You were right there,' said Price.

Jack went on. "On the same occasion I was asked: 'So

you were born in 1958, Mr. O'Neill?' You see I'd filled in the application form inattentively."

Some gaiety floated about in response to this confession.

"But the worst interview happened when I was applying for a secondary school job. I was smart on that occasion, even if the knot on my tie had a peculiar look about it, and I was doing quite well with intelligent answers, when bang! the phone on the table rang. The man in the middle in charge of the interview picked it up with a look of surprise, and there was a crackle of abuse down the line. He said, doing his best to bottle up his astonishment: 'This seems to be for you.' I took the phone, and of course it was Sally on a mission of sabotage – ringing from downstairs at the reception desk. Madness. The game was up. I just got up, said goodbye gentlemen, and went."

More gaiety, in which Jack participated, flowed. But he could not have been in a state of rapture at the time of which he was speaking.

I asked Jack what he considered to be 'well turned out'. It was a cheek of me to ask, but I, in my dapper pinstripe suit, felt in a strong defensive position on the dress code front.

Jack's response was certainly eloquent. 'You may be surprised, but I like the idea of mod clothes, waisted jackets, beautifully cut items of attire, with flowing greens and other bright colours. I'd like to look something like a Spanish grandee – ruffed shirt and so on.'

'You'd get away with it?'

'I doubt others would comment adversely if I carried it off with dignity.'

'Yes?'

Jack paused, and gave an impression that he was returning ruefully to the real world.

'But I have this qualification to make.' He paused again, shaking his head slowly. 'My personality wouldn't fit the clothes. My personality is too much attuned to corduroy trousers, old jackets with reinforcement leather at the elbows, three days' stubble on the chin and the smell of stale beer and piss.'

He delivered these last sentences with zest, and certainly not softly. Bob Hardy, who had been listening alertly, showed amused appreciation. Jack seemed oblivious to signs of disapproval from listeners. Peter Dawlish was holding his pipe a fixed distance from his open mouth for some moments, with a look, I thought, of worldly derision. Oliver Price simply looked ironic, while Stanley Payne (who had joined our seated group minutes before), was looking at Jack as if he were a representative of some version of humankind other than his own.

Shirley Tait and I, on the other hand, simultaneously responded to Jack's contrasting revelations with uninhibited laughter. It was encouraging to observe that Shirley and I had something in common.

13

Suddenly, one evening soon after that stimulating Tuesday, a new dimension was added to my engagement with my further education college world, and, indeed, to my knowledge of the swirl of things outside it. This development was precipitated by my arrival with my evening class register in Mr. Pringle's outer office in the tall main building, moments after my evening class had finished. Another arrival, bearing a similar burden, was Shirley Tait. We deposited our registers almost simultaneously. I then proposed to her, after a moment's consideration, a visit to the Denmark Arms before home-going.

'All right,' said Shirley calmly, 'but it'll have to be quick.'

So we walked over to the pub on the corner where I had at the term's beginning talked with Peter Dawlish and Jack O'Neill. There Shirley insisted on buying the beers after I had failed to get her agreement to my purchase of them. She brought the drinks – a pint for each of us – over to the table I had requisitioned, and our conversation at first was about the students in the classes we had just taken. I soon gathered that one of her students was more intriguing in background than any of mine.

He was, she said, Russian. In those days Russians were rarely to be met with in most people's lives, even in London. So Shirley had been eager for more information. This Russian student, Vladimir, Shirley recounted, was in his late thirties and had told her he lived with fellow Russians, members of the Soviet Trade Delegation, in a large house on Highgate Hill. She had asked what he did in the evenings and he had replied: 'I watch television with my wife.'

Asked if he went out to see plays or films, he had told Shirley that recently the delegation had booked a coach to see, live, the *Black and White Minstrel Show*. (This was a light entertainment production of the time, regularly televised, in which white performers blacked their faces, and enhanced their lips and eyes with white paint to achieve a grotesquely happy caricature of black people. Though the show was offensively discriminatory, more than a decade of complaints was accumulated before it was discontinued.) Shirley had expressed surprise at this choice of entertainment.

'You see,' Vladimir had said, 'many of the wives of delegation members do not speak English, so it was a suitable show for us to see.'

Shirley had asked if some delegation members were women, and he had said some were, but they were a minority. She had decided for reasons of diplomacy not to bring up the subject of the recent Soviet intervention in Czechoslovakia.

It seemed that the lives of Russians in England could be as ordinary as those of many of the natives, and I threw out the idea that the Russian student's trade delegation activities would give him cover as a spy. Shirley was ironic about this. 'I expect there are five MI5 men watching every trade delegation member,' she said. 'Especially when they come to this college for evening classes. I'm probably on their radar for other reasons.'

I looked at her. Her eyes were so blue. She then said: 'I probably shouldn't have said that to you. I am open about my political position, but I don't normally get into staff room discussion about it.'

She looked at me enquiringly. I supposed she was wondering about my own political stance.

'I confess I'm not really that much of a political being,' I explained, 'though I've mixed a lot with left-wingers at university.' I supplemented that by saying, as if inviting personal information – which I was – that I did try to be discreet. I could have added: 'especially when talking with someone I find so attractive.' I said only: 'I assume you're a Red.'

'That's about it,' she said, thrusting her fair hair back with one hand.

'I'd be interested to know what you think about the Czechoslovakia business,' I said. 'Getting to the core of it, do you feel comradely towards those who ordered the troops into Prague?'

'I feel angry,' she said. 'But they obviously believe they are protecting socialism. My own view is that socialism can't be protected in that way in the long run, and that Soviet military action will prove to be counter-productive.'

'I'm sure you're right, but is that the official view of the British CP?'

'Yes, though not the view of all members. There are some who feel they have to support the Soviet Government willy-nilly as if it's always in the right. It used to be axiomatic – the test of your socialism was support for the Soviet Government line. I've not been involved in discussions within the leadership, but I've been a sort of fly-on-the-wall witness in a way.'

'A fly on the wall?' Shirley looked at her half-full beer glass and her watch – which told her it was almost nine-thirty – and I pleaded with her not to leave just yet.

'OK, a later train for me it is,' she said, and she expanded what she had begun to tell me.

'I was working part time at King Street over the summer.'

She didn't need to tell me that this was the head office of the British Communist Party.

'I was helping out there in a practical way,' she said. 'Working there has been an experience.'

'Close to the Covent Garden market?'

'Yes, it's on a corner. It doesn't advertise its presence: but at ground floor level the outside walls are covered by dull green frosted glass. You can't miss it once you know that.'

The Communist Party HQ, she told me, was a place of bare floorboards, and of desks and upright chairs. Shirley went on to say she'd been manning the telephone switchboard in a cubby-hole by the entrance, supplying lines out to Party officials in their offices; putting outside callers through, and also letting visitors in through the inner door (or not as she chose) by pressing a pedal which released the door catch. Visitors first had to show themselves at the open hatch adjoining her perch, and, on identification, she let them through. It had all gone pretty smoothly over the weeks, she said. One or two of the comrades showed irritation when she didn't immediately recognise them and let them through. Most were understanding when this happened.

'Should you be giving me top secret information about security controls?' I asked.

'I'm sure you wouldn't pass it on,' she said, trusting me for whatever reason. 'Anyway the secret police must know all about the building and probably have bugs in it. Not that there's much to be secret about.'

Shirley went on to the most revealing part, to the events while she had been, for a fortnight, stand-in caretaker in place of the permanent husband and wife team, East-enders, who were holidaying in the Soviet Union as 'guests'.

'You were on your own there?' I was incredulous.

'Yes. A woman on her own. I had to convince comrades that I could manage.'

I left that question and found another. 'So were you around in the building when the Russian takeover was announced?'

'I was. I got up that morning without any idea it was happening,' she said. 'I learnt later there had been a grim news announcement – that during the night troops from the Soviet Union, Bulgaria, Poland etcetera, had crossed the Czech frontier.'

'I remember,' I put in. 'The press reports were horrific.'

It was back to Shirley. 'I was about the last to know what had happened. That was a very weird day.'

She took a draught of beer, before continuing. 'Would you like the detail?'

It must have been obvious that I did, as she went on immediately. 'I got up that day at around five thirty. I was sleeping in the flat at the top of the building. I went downstairs to the locked outer iron grill gate. The morning papers were slipped through the grill each day. A small stack of *Morning Stars* was already there. I put these in pigeon holes allocated to various comrades, and I added the other nationals too when they were dropped in, while I was waiting for the office cleaners. The cleaners turned up before long. I let them in, and glanced at the front page of the *Morning Star*. The headline was about a Nazi cache of arms discovered in Chiswick. Nothing at all about the intervention. The paper is put to bed quite early, you see, before the big nationals.'

'What was really funny,' she went on, 'was getting a hint about the intervention through a phone call about a quarter to eight. It was from the correspondent of *Le Monde*. He wanted to speak to the press department to get information about the reaction of the Party to Czechoslovakia....I told him to ring back about nine thirty, me being only the caretaker. I hadn't got an earthly what he was on about.'

Shirley broke off to return to her beer and continued.

'Then a woman comrade came in.'

"Do you refer to each other all the time as 'comrades'?"

'Afraid so,' said Shirley. 'You get used to the language, which after all expresses the fact that you are working with others on the same level for a better world.'

'So what did she say?'

'She said it wasn't much of a day, was it. I thought she meant the weather, and said I hadn't seen much of the day yet. The penny still hadn't dropped. She asked if I'd heard the news – that the Soviet Union had invaded. I could see she was really upset. I was numbed for a minute.'

Sitting there in the Denmark Arms, probably the only pair in the big room talking about the events in eastern Europe, or even about domestic politics, I felt distinctly nearer to the realities of the event. I kept on listening. Our drained beer glasses were removed from our table. I asked how others at the Communist Party's office had responded. She said that some were cracking dark jokes to relieve the tension and the anger.

"One of the youth organisers – he's also quite good on the guitar – asked if anyone had heard of the new song 'We shall Overrun' (a substitute for the Campaign for Nuclear Disarmament anthem *We shall overcome*). Another one pretended to read out an imaginary letter to King Street: 'Dear Comrades, Owing to the Soviet intervention in Czechoslovakia in the cause of world peace and stability, I should like to join the Young Communist League.' The Party's General Secretary, by the way, was climbing up some mountain in Scotland at that moment, and so couldn't be contacted."

Shirley halted for a few moments before continuing. 'Then I noticed an elderly male comrade just arrived, talking with others. He had been in the Party since the year dot, and was talking about serious disaffection in Czechoslovakia, and was justifying the invasion. He wasn't persuading anyone around him that I could tell, and certainly not the youth organisers. That day the Party's press release condemned the military action.'

Shirley paused again, looking at me, and then resumed.

'I was told later on that the elderly comrade who was all for the intervention for once didn't attend his Party branch meeting that month. For him that was unprecedented. He must have felt isolated.'

'But the condemnation,' I said slowly, 'was from a communist party friendly to the Soviet Union. No demonstrations by your lot outside the Soviet Embassy, I expect.'

'True,' said Shirley. 'No apologies for that. But we made our disapproval public.'

I couldn't resist asking Shirley, whose blue eyes I found less resistible than her red politics, if she had spoken to others at the college of these experiences at King Street.

'Only Bob Hardy,' she said. 'He's not in the Party, but we get on politically.'

'I'm still puzzled as to why you have shared all this with me.'

'Well, you're not going to use it against me, are you?'

I wasn't, and I said as much to her. Minutes later we hurried together to the station, and after the short journey to Barking took different trains. I had learned a lot. Off and on, after that, I thought about Shirley. She was a serious as well as a beautiful person. We had not discussed the desirability of radical social change in Britain.

14

October. Colder, wetter, darker times. Winter was coming. The month was sliding past so fast I was hardly aware of its presence. I was getting to work in the mornings on time, and with time to spare despite gloomy skies, but an irritant for me was that Ann Feldman was absent from college a day here and a day there, and that the teacher in charge of municipal accountancy courses – no other than 'Mr. Register' – was pressing me to stand in for Ann on these occasions when her classes didn't clash with my own.

Reg, I could see for myself, was a permanently anxious and deeply reserved man, who, I saw too, became visibly agitated, at least in the case of his municipal accountancy students, if a class register was short of a tick or a cross, or a class of students was without a teacher. If a class within his remit had no teacher standing in front of it because of absence, he was in anguish. But if a substitute, however ill-prepared and ill-equipped for the task, was found to fill the vacant space, it was said that Reg would walk away with a beatific smile on his face. So long as things appeared superficially as they should be, they couldn't be unsatisfactory. Order had been preserved. Fortunately there was a perk for me if I took Ann's classes. I could claim over-time payment, which I did.

Told about Reg's fussiness in the staff room during one morning break, Jack O'Neill expressed sympathy for him. 'It may be,' he said, 'that his demand for impeccable register maintenance was inspired by the exquisite attention to detail in Canaletto's pictures of the Grand Canal in Venice.'

'It's possible,' remarked Peter Dawlish, more taken up with looking at his lecture notes than with listening with care to this nonsense.

Bob Hardy, amused, referred to Reg as 'shudder-making', and the sort of Englishman you could put in a bottle for display on a mantelpiece. Mention was made by Stanley Payne of a chalked message seen on the blackboard of the classroom where Reg had been teaching, announcing that he 'has lesbian tendencies'. Some staff tittered.

Of more interest to me was my sighting, that lunch-time, of Bob Hardy entering the Chinese restaurant near the Denmark Arms with Shirley Tait. I couldn't help considering whether this indicated only that they were friendly as colleagues, or had closer ties than that.

One morning a seventeen-year-old male student in the full time business studies course arrived late for my law class. At the end of the hour he came up to me to apologise and explain his lateness. He had, he said, just passed his driving test, and had driven in through the Town Hall car park gates for the first time, aiming to place his car somewhere inside. He was immediately waved to a halt by the caretaker, who told him rather rudely that only staff, not students, were allowed to park there. I supposed that Peter Dawlish had alerted the caretaker to the need for strict enforcement of the rule.

Not having appreciated the existence of the prohibition, the student had driven to the far end of the car park, intending to turn by the swimming pool building. He had paused, as another vehicle in his path was seeking, but failing, to reverse into a slot effectively, and was for the moment an obstacle to the completion of his own manoeuvre.

Meanwhile the caretaker had zealously followed him on his motor bike (which seemed to have been alertly ready and waiting for deployment), and had ridden up right against the side of the student's car. The driver's side window was wide open, and the caretaker had occupied a lot of the window space with his head. Things had then become confrontational.

'So what did the caretaker do?' I asked.

'He shouted at me to get out of the car and then we'd see what's what. I thought he was probably drunk, so I bopped him on the nose. He withdrew his head from the window.'

'You hit him?' I asked. 'Hit him?' I said again, not quite believing what I was hearing.

I added: 'Full force?'

The student replied: 'Well, certainly enough to make him back off. I don't think his nose bled.' The student's sober facial expression was unchanged. He was articulate, unsmiling, unassuming in manner, and had put to me the case that he had acted solely in self-defence. He added weight to his account.

'If I hadn't hit him, I'm certain he would have assaulted me,' he declared. 'I turned the car round and drove back out, and he was following me on his bike until I was out of the car park. I went straight to the police station and reported him. I thought I'd better do that, because the next person he picked on might not be so able to defend himself.'

It all sounded quite excusable, whatever my initial hesitation. I collected the elements together in my head and repeated the essence to deputy head of department David Fawcett at break time. It was not until the next day when Fawcett came to tell me the caretaker's version of the incident. The caretaker was, I learnt, a Mr. Patience and was married to the canteen manageress. He'd complained personally to Mr. Pringle. He'd said that the student had driven round to park, despite being ordered not to, and had threatened him, saying, allegedly: 'Get out of my way or I'll run you over.' Mr. Patience hadn't apparently thought to mention being biffed on the nose.

In the staff room I passed on to Peter Dawlish the student's account. 'What a cheek,' he said, 'to punch Mr. Patience on the nose and then report him.'

'But if there was provocation?'

'I should think it was the student being provoking,' said Peter. 'A lot of them are getting above themselves this year. It was a public assault.'

Stanley Payne, listening and observing, commented in his low-key way that Mr. Patience had probably been hit because he lacked patience. It was one of Stanley's occasional, if moderately embarrassing, attempts at humour. But he followed this up with the sober comment: 'We could do with a chap like that in the army.'

'Which?' I asked, offering a blank face. 'The student or the caretaker.'

'I think you might guess that the student is in the right age group.'

Peter Dawlish did not join in this part of the conversation. He resumed where he had left off, waving his pipe.

'Students here need keeping in better order. If one of my students is ten minutes late for my class, I tell him that next time he'll have to stay out till the end.'

'And if you're ten minutes late?'

'I pride myself on my punctuality.'

'And on your bow tie,' I thought. Since my last examination of this item, I was sure it had grown larger.

15

Jack O'Neill's child care problems were in time overcome. A nursery for Thomas was found with Town Hall assistance, and only rarely did ructions involving his mad wife Sally occur to such an extent that Jack had to take time off work. One evening I visited him at their Crouch End flat. Sally was still in hospital, but he seemed to be able to meet all demands made on him, while looking more under strain at home than he did at work. I could not avoid noticing that all that evening he wore the blue mackintosh raincoat which he had worn to work that day, although indoors it was neither cold nor raining.

He spoke of his great mistake in buying a flat rather than a house. 'I could have afforded a house,' he said. 'A West Indian couple live upstairs and Sally shouts racialist abuse at them. They've been to the police. There are covenants attached to the lease and I could lose the flat if it goes on. Still,' he went on, 'I believe in taking my disasters one at a time.'

Jack was conspicuously indulgent with three-year-old Thomas. When I pointed this out, he was eloquently without apology. 'He's a motherless babe.' They went on to pull each other's hair, showing something near rapture on both sides.

'You know,' he said, 'When Sally's at home, I have to share a bed both with her and with Thomas. The night is spent fighting over my body. Thomas is a loving little bastard.'

When I left the uncared for maisonette, Jack walked with me, holding Thomas by the hand, to the bus stop, despite the lateness of the hour. He would insist, he said, on seeing me on to the bus. As it happened, the first double-decker to arrive was full and I did not manage to get on it. Yet somehow Jack managed to walk away without observing that I was still on the pavement, waiting for the next one.

I was in the habit of arriving early enough at the college in the mornings to spend a quarter of an hour or more in the well-scrubbed café across the road from the Town Hall annexe. Often I met Oliver Price and Peter Dawlish there. One day they were deep in discussion about the fact that the general certificate results in English at the college were down on the previous year's (due, they told me, to a percentage of random entries which, they averred, distorted the overall result). On another day – for they did not exclude me from their discussions – they told me that a pass in the English exam deserved a higher rating than an equivalent pass in Sociology. I had the sense that there was an invisible partition between their English studies college environment and everything outside it, isolating them, shielding them, validating them. It was in their view a superior article in a sea of mediocre products.

The situation of Ann Feldman seemed not to have resolved itself. She told me one morning, updating her life story without warning as I gathered up books and essay papers:

'I've cleared out of the flat I was sharing with my boyfriend. I've moved in with a girlfriend. My husband says he won't see me again until I've decided whether to go back to him.'

Perhaps it was human, or even inhuman, curiosity that drew me into discussion.

'Do you think you might do that?'

'I think he's changed, better than he was. And our friends think so.'

'But what do your feelings tell you?' I asked recklessly, having the impression that Ann seemed to be too much at the mercy of the views of others.

'I don't feel anything,' she said. 'I've got to collect my clothes. I've hardly got any underwear.'

A moment later Stanley Payne came in, too late, I was confident, to have overheard Ann's admission that her underwear reserves were low. I already had the distinct impression she felt awkward in Stanley's presence, presumably because of his patronising inquisitiveness, and when he came in and sat down, unease was written on her face. She left the room soon after. I saw him again put his hand inside his trousers, leaving it there. I detected no signs of movement on the other side of the fabric.

'What was that about Ann's underwear?' he began. 'Was she hoping you'd check it out for her?'

I remained mute and attempted an expression of severity. He saw that I was looking at his trousers at the point where his hand lay concealed: 'Just playing with myself,' he explained, if inadequately. He delivered an opinion: 'She's only good for one thing, you know.'

'Is that entirely fair?'

'I think she brings out the masculine streak in the day release business studies law class. They'll get across her on the table, if they haven't done already.'

I raised my eyebrows, though in those times I was fundamentally unable to categorise his attitude as constituting root and branch sexism.

After a brief interval, he said reflectively: 'I think she's a bit nympho. She's got to have it regularly. Not necessarily with more than one man. I heard her yesterday talking to her husband over the phone. She was getting soft.'

'She could always commute between the two,' I suggested stupidly.

'I'm not sure she's greedy enough for that, but you never know. Why don't you try your luck?' he suggested.

I felt increasingly uncomfortable about Stanley's misogyny,

even if I did not then so define it. 'When I marry,' I replied, slipping on a coat of simulated worldliness, 'I wish to go to my bride untarnished.'

'I saw that film too,' he replied. The discussion ended there. I was left feeling vexed with Stanley and sad for Ann.

16

I had managed to spend an evening with Marion, the girl I had
met with my university friend Alan in the Gilbert and Sullivan
public house. She immediately remembered me, when I first
telephoned her, and was then both eager and evasive about
making a date for meeting. Twice over the phone she suggested
that we meet the following week without actually fixing on
a defined evening, while proposing that I phone again at
shorter notice. I concede that my delay, in the first place, in
telephoning her may not have helped matters. Anyway, she
at last acquiesced in a jolly way to my proposal at twenty-four
hours' notice of an Indian meal.

Marion shared a rented furnished flat with her friend
Martine somewhere off Clapham High Road, a short walk
from Clapham North underground station. My suit having
ceded place to more casual clothes, I crossed London by tube,
travelling underneath the river, using the Northern line. The
rented flat was larger than mine but as characterless, and with
basic furnishings. Still, it was theirs. Had it been grander, I
might have felt jealous. It had been arranged that I call for her,
and that we would choose an Indian eating place from two
possibilities situated on the High Road.

She was a secretary employed by an agency, as was, she
told me, her friend, moving from one firm to another as
temporary work arose, usually in central London. She had an
engaging smile, a ready laugh and smoked like a chimney. I
refused her offer of cigarettes. She told me in her mild East

Midlands accent that she liked my after-shave lotion. I hadn't seen Alan since the evening in the G & S, but he had visited the flat, I gathered, a number of times.

Even before we sat down to eat in the easily chosen Taj Mahal restaurant, Marion told me that her friend Martine had been sleeping with Alan. Other subjects took over, but during the main course she told me that her friend was no longer involved with him, and she volunteered, with momentary hesitancy, that she had been out with him herself.

'And slept with him?' I couldn't resist asking this, regarding myself as more responsible, or at least more cautious, in sexual relationships than Alan, or, it seemed, Marion. (A year or so previously, a friend of mine had suggested that I was as prudish as the character in C.P. Snow's novels. 'Lewis Eliot?' I responded. 'Not quite, I hope.' Snow's writing, incidentally, features later in this narrative.)

'Well, yes,' she said. 'But he hasn't phoned me lately.'

This was frank enough, if not noticeably diplomatic with regard to me. The conversation was interrupted by a waiter, who told me that the following week the range of dishes on the menu would be extended to include tandoori food. He announced this in a boyish, enthusiastic fashion. I was unwilling to disappoint him by saying no to his request that I inspect the just unwrapped tandoori oven in the narrow corridor which adjoined the kitchen. It was the first time I had heard of tandoori dishes or seen a tandoori oven. When I returned to the table I felt tongue-tied, unable to ask whether Marion, if Alan contacted her again, would then be continuing an affair with him. But it seemed likely enough. We talked of other things, especially of life at work for each of us. The cost of the meal for two was assumed to be mine, and I coughed up the twelve shilling bill, directing a complaint only towards my wallet.

Walking back to Marion's flat, I reached for her hand, and

she pressed mine in return. I was invited in for coffee, but not, she said, for the night. Dithering and disappointed, but remembering too that the next day at college was to be a long one for me, and conscious of the need to be reasonably alert in the morning, I declined coffee politely. I was, as friends told me from time to time, already quite elderly in some of my ways.

We said goodnight to each other in an affectionate way that I interpreted as a sign of possibly good things to come.

I was disturbed by Marion: finding her distinctly desirable; a quality enhanced by her elusiveness. I imagined she liked me; yet it seemed I might be of peripheral significance to her too.

If I was feeling jealous of Alan in relation to Marion, I was even more jealous of Bob Hardy in relation to Shirley. I saw him that week in the college staff car park, where he was getting into the passenger seat of a car in which Shirley was behind the wheel. My one consolation was that she waved at me before they set off.

Not until the following February did I learn of one objective of their car journey: it was to meet with a campaigner for housing for homeless people – a man who supported 'squatting' in unoccupied homes as a way forward, and who might give a talk on this subject to one of Shirley's liberal studies classes. But if I had known that, I would still have been suspicious as to whether there was a second reason for that outing, such as a wish to spend intimate time together.

17

At East Ham I was managing to meet the demands of teaching and preparation for teaching by selectively cutting off corners from the full task; but, as things were, I still did not have much spare time for leisure activities. This was one cause for dissatisfaction; another arose from eruptions of bureaucratic extremism of more than one variety.

As an illustration, I and two others – one was Bob Hardy – each received simultaneously through internal mail a letter from the college librarian threatening legal proceedings for overdue library books. There had been no gentler reminder earlier. 'He's a bastard,' said Bob. 'Ex-Army. He'd personally prefer a drumhead court martial and to administer five hundred lashes; but letters like this are to his great frustration the only sanctions available to him.'

'I'll take the hint,' I said, and soon the books I had borrowed were back in the librarian's custody.

Then I was told one day by David Fawcett that unless the magic figure of fifteen students continued to attend my own weekly evening law class, this would be shut down. He could see I felt deflated, and exasperated on behalf of the students concerned, while I observed with annoyance that he derived satisfaction from my disappointment. As I left him, he provided incontestable evidence for Bob Hardy's assertion that he was 'a nose picker'. One of his narrow, spatular fingers was tunnelling into a vacant nostril, and I decided not to witness the full visitation. As matters turned out, the threat to bring to an abrupt end my evening law class was forgotten, and the course continued, despite the attendance number being down to twelve; but I continued to feel resentment about the handling of the issue.

A similar pantomime, which ended differently, aroused the ire of Stanley Payne, with sympathy from me and others. It concerned a computer analysis course in Stanley's charge, and the 'fifteen students and no less' issue was again very much in the frame. Stanley was told, as I had been, that the course would have to be closed down because fewer than the fifteen who had enrolled were continuing to attend. This decision had been taken although, on enrolment day, students wishing to enrol had been sent away because the required number had been achieved. This class was indeed closed down. It was surely slash and burn at its most mindless in the groves of East Ham academe.

My colleague-in-law Ann continued to attract attention, not always of a disapproving kind. One day she arrived in a dazzling red and blue striped dress. 'What a charming outfit,' said Jack O'Neill, as they passed each other. Bob Hardy was less dignified when he saw Ann. 'Blimey,' he contributed. Ann reportedly showed no reaction to either of these compliments.

She continued to receive communications from her husband in the form of letters and phone messages. The finally lifeless chrysanthemums and the waterless milk bottle had disappeared, and there was no replacement for them.

Then, a couple of days after Ann's appearance in the striped dress, I entered the little room to find her looking ill. She had her face in her hands, and agreed she was in pain.

Stanley Payne came in and jointly we advised her to go home, though Stanley added: 'Or do something', going on to recommend the West End. A distinct lack of compassion was evident beneath the camouflaging words. Ann departed.

Said Stanley to me: 'It's the time of the month, and doesn't she play on it.'

The next day, a Friday, Ann reappeared, looking pale, but behaving 'normally for Ann' by turning up only after her first allocated class – which I had stepped in to take on her behalf. When I saw her at the eleven o'clock break, she looked pale, but seemed otherwise to be coping with the day's trials. Strangely, she then spoke of applying for a more senior post at a west London college, as if such a move could conceivably be a solution to her difficulties. I told Stanley about this plan. His response was characteristic: 'If she gets it, at least she'll be their problem and not ours.'

Ann was increasingly the subject of critical comment from the habitués of the staff room. I was then still feeling out the college culture of what was acceptable and what was not. Of what failings could produce disciplinary steps I was ignorant. Stanley Payne enlightened me.

'They expect one malingerer in a department of this size,' he said, with a weary expression. 'That's why they'll do nothing about Ann, even if she carries on like this indefinitely. At least it should take pressure off Bob Hardy.'

'He's a target of management too?'

'I thought you might have worked that out by now. He does rather ask for it. I've told him to watch out, though when I gave him a friendly warning he was certainly not best pleased.'

Ann had told Stanley she was now back living with her Canadian boyfriend, and on the whole she presented a more cheerful appearance. Still, she seemed to me to have made her life potentially more complicated by having suggested to David Fawcett that her husband, a law graduate like Ann, could assist as a part time teacher to cover an evening class for which a vacancy had suddenly emerged. David Fawcett had, I gathered, conveyed the suggestion to Mr. Pringle, who had authorised this arrangement.

★

Meanwhile, Jack O'Neill's life problems were not solved, and there seemed no prospect they ever would be.

I took over his son's care for an evening. The agreed plan was that I would play with Thomas for a little while in the staff room, then take him home and wait for Jack. This time, the goal of keeping Thomas happy in his father's absence seemed unachievable. Thomas was squalling so loudly that Jack reappeared within a few minutes. Together we took Thomas to the underground station, and then on a train to Barking. There the three of us got aboard the overland train, but Jack, before it set off, escaped on to the platform so that he could get back to the college, leaving Thomas in my sole care.

There followed screams: 'I want my daddy.' But the train had now left the platform without daddy. I produced a sweet. Thomas threw it away angrily. Then another, and another followed, and the anger was replaced by participation in a game. Drawing pictures together followed.

It then occurred to me with horror that Jack had given me no key to his flat. I telephoned the college from a public box after descending from the train at Upper Holloway, and managed, after a minute or two's delay, to get through to him. He said that only the outer door was locked and the couple of Caribbean origin upstairs would let us in. And so it came to pass. We were let in by a friendly black woman, whose demeanour showed unmistakably a soft spot for Jack and for little Thomas. Once inside the neglected ground floor maisonette, Thomas needed a change of underwear and cleaning up, a task which I hesitantly but heroically faced. It struck me that both the lavatory basin and the cooker were in need of a good clean too.

Jack finally arrived to join us, though his arrival was rather later than promised, as he had, through too much concentration on the novel by Balzac (in French of course) that he was reading, and too little on the train's progress, overshot the correct stop. This had not inconvenienced me as Thomas had fallen asleep long before his father returned. When I said farewell to Jack, his head was in the novel. I did not have the heart to draw his attention to the squalor in the lavatory and kitchen.

A week later it was arranged that I would care for Thomas a second time, but when the appointed day arrived, Jack told me that if I went round to the flat, I would find his wife Sally there, though she was not yet discharged as a patient and would have to be back at the hospital by seven. I was unsure what to do, being uneasy at sharing the care of Thomas for any period of time whatsoever with his demented mother, whom I had still not met. But not long afterwards I was let off. A phone call from Jack to the hospital brought the news that Sally need not return there until the following day. So they could survive without my charitable assistance.

At that time Jack seemed more settled in himself, more conscious of what was happening in the college and in the wider world, although beset with the impositions on his energies and emotional resources of a mentally ill wife to whom Thomas's care fell for much of the time when Jack was at work. I watched him in the staff room as he marked essays, pausing, while he considered, at one point, a student's attempt at unconventional abbreviation – 'rembring about anoth'. He scribbled semi-legibly in the margin the comment: 'Mumbling on paper'.

Chatting to me, as he carried on reading and marking, he declared himself, in relation to the contest between expending financial resources on the space race proceeding between Moscow and Washington on the one hand and on the relief of hunger on the other, to be on the side of relieving hunger.

Jack's ability to detach himself from his own life problems enough to express a view in this debate impressed me, but my unease about the ever present risk to Thomas – and therefore to Jack – of Sally's dangerous behaviour remained. I hoped for the best.

18

I had become friendlier, by this time, with Bob Hardy, who, I learnt, taught sociology as well as government. He favoured sports jackets and was usually without a tie. When I saw him on one afternoon occasion wearing a suit – light blue – and a yellow shirt to set it off – he told me this had been his uniform for his most recent job interview, which had taken place not far away at Barking. He had not been the candidate selected.

He was, as he told me, a frequent attender at socialist political meetings, and a participant in anti-apartheid and anti-war demonstrations. He held authority, deference, hypocrisy and opportunism in contempt. He was more than willing to speak his mind publicly in support of this general position, whenever the case for doing so surfaced in his head. Bob, like Peter Dawlish, smoked a pipe. So did another of Bob's bêtes noire, a male colleague who, like Bob, taught government, but, unlike Bob, did so without any hint of radicalism. This colleague was Michael Hastings. Bob reserved some of his most scathing comments for the unfortunate Hastings. 'He's just a bloody prefect,' he declared, 'another Fawcett without the nose picking or the false bonhomie, and the most boring man in the galaxy.'

I had noticed, and several times had exchanged polite conversation with, Michael Hastings. A small and neat man with small and neat features, he was certainly fond of repeating himself. This he did whenever he could escape from intense communion with his pipe, which he did only for the shortest periods of time. He had the appearance in his facial expressions, and in his mannerisms, of a sincere, sensible, dependable, ethical man. He had a voluntary function on the college staff association. He was also endlessly preoccupied, in pleased fashion, with the rise in the value of his mortgaged house. He had told me, at least three times since the term began, that his house was now worth well over six thousand pounds, and he was to tell me the same several times more during the term to follow. He evidently considered himself to be a liberal and fair-minded person, and was considered so by a good number of his colleagues. So much for Michael Hastings.

Bob Hardy was married to a primary school teacher, Diane. I was invited round, one evening when I lacked an evening class, to their flat in Barking. This was situated close to the combined underground and overland railway station, and above a parade of shops. Bob introduced me to Diane, who was taller than her husband, dark-haired, willowy, originated from Lancashire and was as breathtakingly beautiful in my eyes as Shirley, besides having a personality these days often described as feisty. She also said sensible things for which Bob reproved her in my presence, telling her she was being dull. Dullness wasn't a weakness with which I was prepared to endow her.

It was Diane who cooked chops and vegetables in the kitchen, while Bob and I motored our way rapidly through a bottle, or possibly two, of cheap red wine. As usual we discussed colleagues, and I told him about Michael Hastings's contented references to the current value of his house.

'When he tells me about it,' said Bob, 'I generally say that I'm sure that's less than he told me last time. He's fairly slow to rumble when he's being got at.'

'Conversation in the staff room can be dull,' I remarked.

'You know,' said Bob, 'I've never heard a single general discussion about education in the staff room. Not one. Nothing outside closed concepts, nothing outside attendance, marks, standards, examination papers and what not. The intellectual standard is at best Civil Service clerical officer class level, and probably a couple of measures lower.'

'Maybe Civil Service clerical officers would do better,' I agreed. But Diane and the chops joined us, and more wine and conversation followed, but I had already drunk more than I should have done, and most of the conversation did not fix itself in my memory. I had decided in advance not to refer to Shirley during the evening, in case it created awkwardness, and I stuck to this intention. Bob did not do so either.

I remember, though, that I said at one point that Bob's readiness to open his mouth in the department's staff rooms was refreshing. Diane took this up and observed that Bob was ready to open his mouth anywhere. She went on to say that when she'd returned from staying with her parents in Lancashire a couple of years before, Bob had immediately blurted out that he'd been going out with someone else when she'd been away. Bob did not seem perturbed about this revelation.

'We all have our ups and downs.'

'Now you're being dull,' Diane retorted. 'As well as drunk.' By this time I would myself have openly admitted to both deficiencies. Soon after I departed homewards, remembering little of that journey the next day, but remembering much about the impression Diane had made upon me.

However beguiling I found Diane, and however incomprehensible that Bob should have in the past risked his relationship with her for the sake of a casual liaison, I was still far more bewitched by Shirley. It followed that I continued to be troubled by the thought that Bob might be conducting an extra-marital affair with her. And though Diane seemed well able to stand up for herself, was she nevertheless, I wondered, so committed to her marriage to Bob that she would not walk out on him if he was indeed behaving adulterously?

The next day, bumping into Shirley in the corridor in the annexe, I gave myself the chance to find out more, and to get to know her better, by proposing another drink in the Denmark Arms – or wherever she chose.

'I'm a bit tied up for the next week or so,' she said. 'Ask me again.' I masked and nursed my disappointment, and tried to be philosophical.

19

October was well advanced, and the weather was certainly deteriorating. At home I had a paraffin stove, which could be put to use to supplement my tinny two bar electric fire, but it suffered the disadvantage that its wick needed renewing. I didn't purchase a new wick or complain to my landlady, and decided to manage without it, however cold the weather became. I would be snug enough.

One evening I phoned Marion. She answered the phone and said immediately:

'I thought you weren't going to phone.'

'Of course I was. What about Friday evening?'

'That would be lovely. Why don't you come round for a meal. I could cook for you.'

I had not bargained for her enthusiasm. After a moment I said that sounded wonderful.

'Come about eight,' she said.

I did not demur. This sounded too good to be true.

So that Friday evening, having no car, I made my way to Marion's, once again, via the Northern underground line. She was, when she opened the door, more attractive than I had remembered from our first evening together. Fairly slim, not very tall, dark haired, full lipped and laughing. And smoking incessantly. We spent no time in the badly lit hallway beyond our warm initial greeting. Marion's friend had already gone away for the weekend.

Before long we were sitting down to eat whatever it

was she had cooked, washed down with a bottle of white wine (not quite the very cheapest), which I had brought as my contribution. I confess I hardly noticed what I ate, but congratulated her on her cooking. She lit up a cigarette and for once I took one from her. There was desultory chat about her work and mine, and she said suddenly, after a long drag at a cigarette:

'Why don't we go to bed early.'

We did, and the experience seemed to disappoint neither of us. At one moment she said, with a giggle, that we could have 'done it' when I had said 'no' to coming in for coffee.

She had only, she said, wanted me to avoid staying the night on that occasion. I had not read the signs correctly.

Marion was now my post-University girlfriend. But for how long? Was this the end as well as the beginning? I was not optimistic, partly because I sensed that for Marion I might be a convenient gap-filler, and partly because I was beginning to have real, if unrealistic, hopes that Shirley might for me put an end to all gaps in my own romantic life.

20

The second half of October was honoured by a betrothal between the glamorous widow of an assassinated American President and an elderly Greek shipping magnate of far from handsome appearance, and by the televised excitement of athletics finals in the Olympic Games in Mexico. A Kenyan man took the 1500 metres final in brilliant style, and an Ethiopian seized the marathon title; while the three fastest Americans – all black men – in the 400 metres final amazed the world when they appeared on the medals' presentation podium. Wearing black berets and raising clenched fists, they expressed their feelings about the Vietnam war and the situation of black people in their country, precipitating their immediate recall home. Not long afterwards, in a different sort of competition, spacecraft put into orbit by the Soviet Union attracted much public attention.

While my own eyes at that time were in part drawn to the track events in the Olympic Games, others at the college were more absorbed by the antics of 'the athletes in space'. Oliver Price was a committed member of this group.

A major anti-Vietnam war demonstration in London was due before the end of the month, and one of the 'Ad hoc Committee' organisers was reported to be a young Pakistani intellectual and socialist, answering to the name of Tariq Ali. Alarming stories were appearing in the press as the month advanced, claiming that violence was planned by the demonstrators. Press reports spoke of the preparation of

Molotov cocktails and of the proposed 'takeovers' of 'strategic places' by demonstrators, and these lurid stories were to lead to the closure of museums and art galleries on the day of the event. In East Ham a local Conservative Parliamentary candidate called for a ban of the rally, while a sitting Conservative MP from elsewhere called for legislation which would enable the deportation of 'foreign scum', a category which patently implied the inclusion of Tariq Ali, from Britain's shores.

After a few days of relative warmth in mid-month, I found myself digging out from a partly broken bedroom drawer the string vests I had not worn since the previous winter. One morning, upon waking, I saw mist through my window, and when I emerged from East Ham underground station and began the High Street walk to the college, visibility was below fifty yards. The outer world was closing in, and the fog was to be a background presence in London for days. In this confining world, I spent evenings at home, preparing for lessons and marking essays, often with one of my landlady's cats near enough to lick my face, an occupation which I tolerated reluctantly, but which the cat seemed to relish.

The annual college staff social, which took place conveniently just after the days of fog had passed, I boycotted. The customary ballroom dancing did not appeal to me for one thing, and when later I heard feedback in the staff room about this unfashionable event, my relief that I had dodged it was vast. At some stage in the evening, I was reliably informed, the *Okey Cokey* dance was performed. Such occasions were not, I felt, 'my scene', though I was told that the Principal, Mr. Plummer, put store by the occasion, and that staff who attended were in consequence more highly regarded by him. They had elected to be members of his circle, at least for the evening.

Ann Feldman had steered clear of the social too – perhaps for different reasons. Her absences for indisposition were accumulating – eight or nine days so far, I calculated, with ample opportunities for more during the balance of the term. She declared herself unwell, but the specifics of her illness were not confided to me, directly or indirectly. Peter Dawlish told me – though how he knew he didn't say – that on a day when she had succeeded in attending the college, she sent a day release class home early so that she could go to a football match with her Canadian boyfriend.

Even Mr. Pringle, buried in his room, was said to have commented that Mrs. Feldman was regularly the first to go down with things. Stanley Payne, having heard about this, said he thought she went down a lot with or without things. David Fawcett, making one of his occasional forays into the staff room, was also forward, as well as moralistic, in his assessments. 'I may be old-fashioned,' he said, hearing Ann's name mentioned, 'but I've always thought there should be a limit to the number of husbands you have.'

Bob Hardy, sipping coffee, looked at David Fawcett intently at that moment, saying nothing, and Fawcett went on, changing tack: 'You can joke about it, but she has a heck of a problem.'

Bob relaxed a little but continued to say nothing. Fawcett left, and Bob told me of a stand-up corridor row he had had with Dai Griffiths, the liberal studies chief, who had berated Bob for being late for a class although he, Griffiths, had no management function in relation to Bob's work.

'I told him straight,' said Bob, 'that he should be in his office if he didn't have any teaching to do, at least pretending to work. I said that from what I had heard, his own name was a by-word for sloth.'

Oliver Price, who had been listening, crossed his legs and inhaled deeply the smoke from his untipped cigarette, then remarked:

'I'm sure you were in the right, but you do yourself

sometimes give the impression, Bob, and I hope you won't take offence at my saying so, of being a consultant here – arriving without haste, disgorging a few pearls of wisdom, glancing at your watch and departing at a convenient moment.'

Bob laughed at this amiable sally. He seemed untroubled by the absence of prospects of promotion. Or by the prospect of severe management displeasure in consequence of his routine disregard of bureaucratic expectations.

21

Twice over two or three days in October's third week I phoned my university friend Alan to arrange a drink or a meal somewhere, but either he wasn't answering his telephone or he wasn't in to answer it. I phoned a third time and this time he answered, and in jaunty mode. I decided not to risk embarrassment by making reference to either of the two women we had met in the Gilbert and Sullivan, and we arranged to meet at the very same beer-drinking site. Wearing a conventional overcoat in the colder weather, I was the first to arrive.

After Alan's entry a few minutes later, 'Light ale goes with light opera', was his first comment, as well as containing his drinking preference for the evening. He promptly removed the beige duffle coat of which I knew he was extremely fond. As we talked I studiously avoided references to the two girls, Alan's escapades with each of them in sequence, and the progress to date of my involvement with Marion. Alan was not one to gossip about sexual adventures: he just got on with them. He always seemed more interested in the next one than in the last one, or (a mutual friend had once cynically suggested to me), than the present one. I did not ask either about his long suffering satellite girlfriend, who often seemed depressed, perhaps because of the state of her relationship with Alan, perhaps because she never expected anything better.

I did express curiosity, though, about how he was getting on with his international law studies. 'It's O.K.,' he said unenthusiastically. 'It's less political than I expected. The Professor is very authoritarian, a Stalin in democratic clothing. I grit my teeth to avoid antagonising him. I'm feeling my way.'

Alan regaled me with a picture of the master's degree international law course to which he was now committed, and of some of the people concerned.

'I hadn't realised the student composition would be so mixed. There are Greeks, Canadians, Americans, a German, Africans – only a handful of English students. A lot of them are bought and paid for by rich law practices or governments. I'm a poor relation.'

'So I suppose it's not full of socialists. What about the lecturers?'

'The Professor at University College is Georg Schwarzenberger,' said Alan. He had pronounced the forename as 'Gayorg'.

'The name doesn't mean anything to me.'

'I wish it didn't to me,' said Alan. 'His name's on half the textbooks. He's a reactionary little swine. Though I think a lonely little swine too. Not many allies, except a few that suck up to him.'

'And the ethos generally?'

'Well,' he said. 'It's got a rather elite feel to it. The seminars aren't called seminars. A seminar is a colloquium – or the word is colloquia if you want the plural.'

'That seems to imply a sharing of view-points.'

"When Georg Schwarzenberger is leading the colloquium, only one view-point gets shared. His. Apart from when you hear his voice, it's a pretty silent debate. He's great at putting you in your place. 'What sort of authority do you call that?' he barks out, if you tell him something from some over-elementary text book. 'You are not informing,' he says when you do your best to contribute, but are saying something too commonplace. Funny thing, though, he'll talk to anyone.

He'll come up and drink coffee with you in the cafeteria, make small talk with you, but it's pretty much of a monologue in which there's not much room for any view but his own. It's an alternative colloquium. A monoloquium."

'I'm glad we haven't got him at East Ham. He sounds like someone you can do without.' I had a suggestion for Alan. 'What about taking into a colloquium one of the Professor's textbooks, but with a fake cover on it bearing the words 'A Child's Introduction to International Law'. When he laughs at it with the most lordly contempt, you just need to flip off the cover and show him his own book.'

'I'll bear that in mind,' said Alan, who was keen to tell me more about his obnoxious professor. "I met him just after the start of term. I was waiting for someone, when this little man, early sixties, walked quickly up to where I was hovering in the corridor. He asked who I was waiting for. I just said: 'Who might I be speaking to?' He said who he was and who was he speaking to? I told him and that I was on the international law course. 'So who are you waiting for?' he said again. 'I don't like to see students wasting their time.'"

Alan swallowed light ale and resumed his tale.

"I said I hoped it wasn't a waste of his time occupying himself with such matters, saying this with a pleasant expression, of course. He looked back at me, not in the least affronted, and said: 'So who are you waiting for?' I gave in prevaricating at that point and gave him the answer he wanted. He's like a dwarf bulldozer."

I thought of Fawcett, of Pringle, of Plummer, even Dai Griffiths, but all these were straw monsters, if monsters at all, in comparison. Schwarzenberger, I could see, would gobble them up one after the other for breakfast, like mouthfuls of porridge. He would make a terrifying substitute for all of them. A troll under Senate House's bridge, waiting for students – or subordinate staff – to appear. This was a different world to mine.

Only later it struck me that Alan's self-righteous exasperation was misplaced: the Professor's brusque corridor interrogation was intended to help, not to bully. As it was, I just asked how the Professor got on with other students.

"Just last week a Tanzanian student spoke up, referring to the exploitation of African countries. Schwarzenberger ignored that. But he asked the student where he'd been studying, and it came out that he'd been studying the law of revolutionary warfare at Moscow University. Schwarzenberger looked at him and said in a brutal way: 'Here, you will have to unlearn everything you learnt there.'"

'That ended that exchange,' Alan rounded off, and my meeting with him had nothing else of importance to say for itself.

Although Shirley was by her own account too busy to spare time for a drink with me, I did arrive one morning in the 'over the road' café when she was half-way through her own breakfast-time refreshment. We had a few minutes' conversation. No one else from the college fraternity was present, and I asked Shirley if she was still helping out at Communist Party headquarters.

'Not much,' she said. 'The looming big anti-Vietnam war march is the thing at the moment.' She had, she said, a small part in organising it, especially recruiting stewards for the event. Including dock workers.'

'Dockers?' I asked.

'Dockers,' she said. 'I won't tell you why.' I was to learn the reason much later.

I asked if she anticipated there would be the mayhem anticipated by the press, and she said she was sure that if there was, it would be a minority activity. The Party and the mainstream CND movement would be disciplined and responsible, she anticipated, and she hoped the police would be too.

I seized the opportunity to suggest we exchanged phone numbers, and Shirley was willing to provide hers.

Though tempted to take part in the march, I knew my motivation would be too much to impress Shirley, so I decided to be ethical and to stay away. Was another reason that I feared, influenced by the media-spread rumours, that there might be some great battle with the police, and that I wished to keep out of harm's way?

Overwhelmingly peaceful and unquestionably huge that march of Saturday 27 October 1968 proved to be. Only a smallish group of demonstrators, I read in the Sunday newspaper next day, had peeled off to confront the American Embassy in their own manner. Shirley was to tell me later – recalling with amusement a detail she had observed during the march – that an anarchist group must have been responsible for a large anti-police slogan on a wall which read:

'FUCK †HE FUZZ'.

Instead of marching against war that Saturday I went shopping with the intention of acquiring a second suit, preferably made to measure. Looking into a shop window where women's clothing was draped on tailor's dummies of women, I was struck by the fact that the dummies were remarkably sexually explicit beneath underwear – it was not a feature I had seen previously. In a large chemist's, one of a chain, I saw, again registering something new, that a security camera eye operating through a diving-suit-style helmet was on the alert to catch thieves. It was my first conscious sighting of a pioneer of the closed circuit TV systems which today are almost everywhere. But then, I wasn't an avid shopper.

The suit I bought that day pleased me, though I settled for an off-the-peg item with minor adjustments to the length of the trousers. It was, I decided, in an expression of the time, a pretty cool set of threads. I now had two almost identical dark pinstripe suits: one brand new and one I had acquired the previous summer. I was equipped to meet the world head-on.

Wending my way home by bus, I was exposed to the noisy but not aggressive antics of two youths who shared the upper deck with me. Their departure from the bus as it approached the junction of the Holloway Road with Upper Street was both loud and rapid. One of them responded to the sight of a male acquaintance on the pavement on the far side of the road by bellowing through the upstairs window the friendly greeting of 'Wanker!' The pair then descended the stairs with a clatter and jumped off the platform in rapid succession while the bus was still moving.

What would I do, I asked myself, if I were addressed from the upper deck of a bus by a friend in such a colloquial manner? Amused, I thought of the line from one of Raymond Chandler's stories: 'Down these mean streets a man must walk'. I thought too of Jack O'Neill's early classification of me as resembling a minor public school tyke. I was a middle class product with middle class language and attitudes. There could be no mistake about that.

The following day, unexpectedly, Alan phoned me to say he proposed to offer his services as a part time teacher at East Ham – either in sociology or law. He said he'd posted a letter to Mr. Pringle, while not expecting anything to come of it. I wished him luck with his application, while saying I didn't know of any vacancies at the moment. Though tempted to express my disapproval of his having got involved with Marion, involvement continuing or not, I desisted. In truth, I did not want to ruffle the waters of my friendship with Alan. Some day I might say something short of approval of his behaviour.

22

Part of me regretted that I had not taken part in the anti-Vietnam war march which filled central London streets at the weekend in late October. I awaited an opportunity to hear from Shirley her own account of the event.

Meanwhile cold weather filled the air formidably for weeks. I went out with Marion on more occasions, enjoying her cheerfulness, her lively conversation about events in her daily life, and our time in bed together. I could have done without her extensive cigarette smoking, but was too polite to make adverse comments.

She had a sharp and observant eye for the universe around her, and a knack of telling a story in a way that always drew me in. She had ceased temporary work and was now based in the head office of a major company manufacturing printing equipment as personal assistant of a regional customer advice department manager. A 'CAD' manager, she called him.

'When I started there a week ago,' she told me, 'I was given a quick tour round the offices, and introduced to about twenty people. The girl taking me round told me there were some you had to salute, and one or two you had to drop a curtsey to.'

'In a manner of speaking,' I suggested.

'At the end of the first week,' she said "one of the engineers came in to talk to my boss. They were chatting and then the engineer got a bit heated. He said to my boss: 'I've never worked in a firm with so many crawlers. I've seen people crawl to you. I've seen you crawl to the company secretary and I've seen him crawl.'"

'Did your boss like that?'

'Guess. And he didn't like it in front of me, either. Though I get on with him ever so well. He says he likes my Nottingham accent.'

I dared not ask Marion if she was sharing her bed with other boyfriends too. Or even with her boss. She spoke in a very matter of fact way about sex, seemed to have been free and easy in her relationships. I decided to live for the moment, and not trouble myself about whether my time with her had an early finishing date.

During this time the US Presidential election, like the anti-Vietnam war march, came and went. A newspaper headline happily announced: 'Yes – Nixon's the one'. So, as it was presented, the more war-like Republican candidate Nixon, faced with the on-going war in Vietnam, had defeated the supposedly less war-like Democratic Party candidate Hubert Humphrey. Not knowing much about the candidates or their politics myself, I was still able to spot even greater innocence of useful knowledge on the subject amongst some of my colleagues.

In the staff room, a lithe and bright eyed young woman, a physical education teacher, sought basic information. 'Who's a hawk and who's a dove?' she asked.

Bob Hardy attempted to explain. 'They are both hawks,' he declared, as if the matter was self-evident. 'They are both Wall Street Cold Warriors.' The woman's name, I was told, after she had departed, was Irene. I could see from her facial expression that she did not feel much enlightened. I decided too that she was extremely attractive, and feared that I would never get to know her.

'I'm sure it'll be all right,' said Oliver Price, referring to the American election outcome.

'What you mean is,' said Bob Hardy firmly, 'it's eleven o'clock in the morning, life feels quite good, you're fully awake and on top of things, and the world ought to be in good shape too. You're just a natural optimist. This nasty, disgusting war is going to go on, and more people in that far off country are going to die.'

'You may be right,' said Oliver Price, 'Or perhaps you're just a natural pessimist. Anyway, I must confront my class.'

After he left us, I suggested to Bob that Oliver saw himself very much as old wood. Bob said to me that in his book old wood usually equated to new fascism. He added quietly: 'Oliver's quite well fixed, you know. His wife's a head teacher at a primary school. Between them they can't be on less than five thousand. No children.'

'Does five thousand a year automatically produce an optimistic Conservative?' I asked.

'No,' replied Bob. 'But it can help you to feel comfortable and complacent. And help you to feel, if you needed any encouragement, that your future is tied into Establishment perceptions of the world.'

'Mm,' I commented.

A vivid memory sails back to me of a return home after an evening out with Marion at that time. In the street, not far from her Clapham home, walking ahead of me, was a very old man, half keeled over, fixed in position, carrying in one hand a brown paper parcel tied with string, and a brown shopping bag in the other, shuffling along, presumably going home, wherever home might be. It was so evident that he had so little future, yet had so much determination. If I pitied, I also respected and admired.

For a week or more, in the second half of November, I did not see Marion, though I phoned her several times. Once I spoke to Martine, her flat mate, and left a message, to be passed on, that I had rung. One evening, when Martine had told me Marion would be at home, I phoned twice, letting the phone ring and ring, but there was no answer. I wondered if I had been dismissed without words of dismissal, and felt put out. I suspected that I might have a successor, and if so, would have preferred to have been told. And yet I could hardly say my liaison with Marion had that much going for it. I postponed phoning her again for a few days, not wishing to be thought of as pursuing her.

Enoch Powell was again in the news for another speech on the subject of race. His anticipations of conflict between whites and blacks, and his anecdotal evidence of intimidation of the former by the latter, were the subject of sharp analytical condemnation in a serious newspaper or two, and of praise for his humanity and wisdom in the gutter sheets. Not long after, a satirical magazine produced a front page picture of Powell apparently measuring the air, a spread of a foot or so, the caption offering his supposed words:

'And some of them have got them that long.'

I heard no more talk of Powell in the staff room. Those who had some sympathy with him were keeping their heads down.

Christmas selling in the shops, which were decorated accordingly, had begun. Ann Feldman was now absent from work again. A back-dated doctor's certificate, underwriting her sickness absence for two weeks, reached David Fawcett, and in the staff room he rubbed his hands together and suggested she had her GP in the palm of her hand.

'Or on top of her,' said Stanley Payne.

On form that day, Jack O'Neill, who had been listening intently, said that Stanley was obsessed by sex, which though pleasurable, led to having a bad back and financial difficulties.

A colleague who was not au fait with the twists and turns

of Ann's personal life chipped in to say that he'd asked Ann's husband (who was now teaching an evening class at the college once a week), when she'd be back, and he'd said 'Next week'. After this colleague had gone, Stanley commented: 'It's anyone's guess whether her husband would know that, since he's not living with her at the moment, so far as we know. But I suppose he likes, being her official husband, to pretend to the public he does know about her comings and goings.'

It was then that the oldest member of the teaching staff, who contributed to the training of bookkeepers on a part time basis, a man with an established reputation for being, at the very least, a little out of step with his colleagues, piped up. He looked over at me and introduced the subject of my law teaching predecessor, he of mimicry fame:

'The man in your job before you.'

'What about him?' I said, 'A man in a hurry.'

'He was bent, wasn't he?'

I said nothing. 'Well he wasn't married, was he?'

Neither I nor anyone else answered. The question was left to float. This staff room conversational contribution I could not have invented.

I did doubt, though only for a few seconds, whether a dull piece of recent college history, told me in an amused manner by Bob Hardy, who had absolutely no inclination for imaginative invention, could be completely authentic. Until this year, he said, there had been an annual autumn prize-giving in the college for full time students, presided over by the Principal.

'A prize-giving?' I asked with incredulity. 'As if this place is a grammar school?'

'Certainly.'

Though attendance at the prize-giving in the autumn of the previous year had been small, the occasion was, said Bob, planned with care and formality. Peter Dawlish had been put in charge of stewarding for the purpose of showing visitors to their seats, putting the right people on the platform and so on. Bob too, and a couple of others, had been press-ganged into assisting Peter. 'I should have objected,' he said. 'I don't support pats-on-the-back-for-being-a-good-sea lion events.'

Bob went on to say that he had dutifully turned up, but that even before Mr. Plummer stood up to introduce the evening to a hall mostly empty of prize winners and their supporters, he and the other stewards, Peter included, had sloped off to the Denmark Arms. None of them had been present for the actual distribution of prizes. In the pub Peter had got a bit drunk and confided to Bob he was beginning to regret being engaged to be married. 'So far as I know,' said Bob 'nothing was said later to Peter Dawlish upbraiding him or anyone else for decamping early.'

The whole thing had been evidently more of a damp squib than a thumbs-up applause for excellence. The formerly annual event, however, had now ceased without any accompanying announcement. No prize-giving was to be held this year. There was simply no arrangement for continuation. It had become too embarrassing an occasion, and had been unobtrusively dropped from the calendar.

23

Out of the blue a phone call from Shirley arrived at my home during my journey there from East Ham. My landlady had taken a message for me to return the call right away, and I did just that. Shirley then told me she had a spare ticket for a Guyanese music event at the Festival Hall the next day. She called it *Guyana Johnny*. Would I go with her?

I had nothing special fixed, so gratefully agreed. But perhaps I would have agreed anyway. The next evening found me crossing the footbridge across the Thames to the Festival Hall. Shirley was at a table in the self-service café in the long stretch alongside its windows, as she had said she would be. She was stirring a cup of tea and staring out at the dark waters, and the passing boats and pedestrians. When she saw me, she waved, and insisted on going off to get me coffee.

Her return to the table was followed by an apology from her for the short notice of the invite to me.

'I can guess,' I said. 'Someone dropped out. But that's all right.' I was sure that the 'someone' would be Bob Hardy.

I was right. Shirley, looking embarrassed, explained that he had first accepted, then withdrawn, after receiving some sort of ultimatum by Diane. 'He's been neglecting her, I gather,' said Shirley.

I decided not to add: 'In favour of yourself?'

The event was to be in the Purcell Room and we walked over there soon after, meantime gossiping about colleagues and the college.

I had assumed there would be live music, but none was forthcoming. Instead there was, on the dais, a table on which sat proudly a mammoth tape recorder, equipped with two large horizontal reels. Next to it stood a jug of water and a drinking glass. I inferred that the intention was to play us something, and observed that there were not a great many people in the hall. In fact, there were very few: twenty or twenty five at most, making me think of the poorly attended prize-giving at the college the previous year. No printed programme was being distributed.

Shirley explained to me that portions of an opera by the communist composer, Alan Bush, would be played. It was *The Sugar Reapers*, otherwise known as *Guyana Johnny*. It relied on indigenous Guyanese folk tunes to a large extent, and had never been performed in Britain. The only European production had been in Leipzig, in Communist East Germany (or in the German Democratic Republic as Shirley put it).

On to the platform walked a man in late middle age. He was ruggedly handsome, and wore a baggy suit. I had the impression (which would have been solidly reinforced if Wellington boots had replaced his shoes), that he might be a gentleman farmer. He was, said Shirley, Chairman of the Communist Party's Music Group.

'Is this a subtle – or possibly an unsubtle – ploy to recruit me?' I asked her jokingly.

She disclaimed with a smiling negative. 'It's to enhance your knowledge of music, celebratory music, concerning ordinary people in the third world. And mine too.'

The Chairman was clearly waiting for something, perhaps for more audience members to arrive, and I saw that more seats were occupied now, perhaps sixty or seventy in all. The speaker, who now joined the Chairman on the low stage, was formally introduced, and proved to be none other than the composer Alan Bush himself. I guessed however, and correctly as it turned out, that because this was an event open to the public, the term comrade was not to be used that day and there was no spoken reference to the Communist Party.

Alan Bush, who looked to be in his sixties, cut a formidable figure. In size he was colossal. He towered over the record player table. His speaking voice was sonorous, he had a domed forehead, and when excerpts were played from *The Sugar Reapers*, his head was cocked on one side, completely taken up by the music. He introduced an excerpt, played it (hovering over the tape recorder like an elderly but still enormously powerful eagle), and then delivered observations before moving on to the next piece to be played. When he needed to, he stabbed with precision and speed at the 'stop' or 'start' button. During this procedure, repeatedly he removed his hands from his pockets and replaced them, and as frequently began the process of sitting down before leaping up again in mid-movement. I was entranced by the man as much as by his music.

As the session moved towards a close – there was no interval – the composer told us of the unsuccessful efforts made to get the opera performed in Britain. There were several questions from audience members about the problems of obtaining live performances, and only one about the composition process. Bush declared, in answer to this question, that he had been deeply influenced by the folk music of Guyana, and had not felt at all inhibited from including themes derived from this music in his work. Questions done, the Chairman gentleman farmer, apparently forgetting that he was not presiding over an internal Communist Party debate, declared 'the meeting' closed.

As we got up to go, I was startled to recognise an East Ham colleague. He had been sitting a few rows behind me. He was the only black teacher in the department, in fact a liberal studies teacher, and I guessed he must be of Guyanese origin, which indeed proved to be the case.

'This is unexpected,' he declared. 'I didn't know you had an interest in Guyana.'

'I was roped in by Shirley,' I replied, turning to Shirley who had been standing just behind me. But she was now some yards away, talking energetically to a young black woman who was standing in the aisle. My colleague had a gentle and pleasant manner, and spoke English without any distinguishing accent. I asked him how he got on with other staff in the department, and he said he had no problems with anyone, but also described himself as a bit of a loner. 'I don't socialise much,' he said. Shirley came over to us, and greeted our mutual colleague with warmth.

The three of us then headed for the narrow old footbridge adjacent to the enclosed railway lines across the river, which I had crossed earlier in the opposite direction. The ugly back end of Charing Cross railway station faced us. Part way across, we paused for a few seconds to stare city-wards, identifying the cathedral of St. Paul in the distance. Darkness and the city united with the bleak swirling waters passing underneath to produce a harshly romantic prospect. Below on the water was flotsam – scraps of paper, wood and less easily identifiable floating debris.

Shirley and I parted from our colleague, who declined our invitation to join us for a drink, on the north side of the river, and we drifted over, on my suggestion, to the Gilbert and Sullivan public house. As we were about to enter, Shirley said with a grin that she would obviously have preferred having a drink at the 'Shostakovich' or the 'Prokofiev', or even the 'Alan Bush', but would not put up a fight about the choice of venue, especially as it brought back carefree memories of singing in G & S operas at school.

I chose the table I had sat at before with Alan. Shirley looked at the framed music of *For he is an Englishman* on the pillar nearby, deprecated cheerfully its male gender-weighted patriotism, and proposed the substitution for the original of the words 'For she is a Socialist'. I chuckled. This time Shirley accepted that I buy the drinks.

Said she, when I brought two brimming beer glasses over to our table: 'I get the impression that you keep out of political involvement.'

'Point taken. I'm hardly unique. But I'd like to hear about your experience of the anti-Vietnam war march. I was there in spirit.'

'It was like any anti-war march, but much, much bigger than the usual thing. When I got to the start, at Embankment, close to the tube station, in fact where we've just been walking, thousands were already there, and there weren't as many police as I expected. Before I worked my way into it, I saw that Pakistani bloke with a moustache at the front.'

'Tariq Ali?'

'Spot on. Death threats made against him had been phoned to the organisers, and King Street made sure he had some protection.'

'Oh.'

'In the form of some brawny dockers.'

'You told me previously you were recruiting them.'

'So I did.' She drank some beer, as I did. 'That just meant a phone call to a dockers' leader. But he didn't need a bodyguard as it turned out. The police behaved well on the main march, and in Hyde Park from what I could see. There were masses of police in Whitehall, as if they were expecting an attack on Downing Street. What I hadn't expected was such a big turnout of marchers. Especially of students.'

'TV and the papers didn't report big numbers.'

'If there weren't huge numbers – the National Council of Civil Liberties reckoned 100,000 – could you explain how it took hours for everyone, stretched across the road, to enter Hyde Park? It's been a very long time since we've had a march in London as big as that. And it was friendly. Because of the fear of being attacked, we were marching a lot of the time with linked arms across the width of roads.'

'Inspiring?'

Shirley looked at me and paused. 'For me, yes. And I think for a lot of others.'

'The papers concentrated on reporting what happened outside the US embassy. Arrests.'

'Yes, but that was quite a small group – Maoists, anarchists, wanting to act in a provocative way. Not that there were that many arrests.'

I was feeling acutely that I should have been on the march with Shirley. And with the thousands who did march. And as the conversation progressed, the environment became less of a London pub and more of a tutorial room, in which G & S operas did not feature as subject-matter for discussion. Our beer glasses emptied gradually.

'So do you think the march will make much difference to whether the Vietnam war will end?' I asked.

'In itself, of course not. It gave more of a signal to our government than to the Americans. How the war will end will depend much more on what happens in America and in Vietnam itself. I just point out one thing.'

'Go on.'

'In this country the message is put into every home, remorselessly, on TV and in the papers, that the Soviet Union is a military threat to the West, and that America is our protector. Protecting us somehow in Vietnam. Some of that message sticks. Yet how much evidence is produced that we are threatened?'

'You would say nil.'

'Well, you find some, and tell me about it. They point to the fact that Russia has nuclear bombs – yes, but they acquired those a few years after America dropped two on Japan. They point out that Russia put nuclear missiles in Cuba – yes, but only to help Cuba resist a threatened invasion in 1962, after a failed invasion earlier. The missiles were removed and the invasion was cancelled. The war with Germany was a hundred per cent defensive on Russia's side with vast casualties. Russia isn't going to start another one now.'

I was ready enough to accept this, while not anxious to do much about spreading the message. I moved the discussion on. 'The West does make a great deal out of spy scandals and what-not, though, doesn't it?'

'I agree. The unspoken argument seems to be that if they're spying on us, they must have some malign intentions. But we spy too, even if their spies have been better placed than ours.'

'Philby and co'.

'Exactly.'

'I've been reading,' I contributed, 'in the papers, that it's finally coming out that the escape of spy George Blake from his 42-year sentence to the Soviet Union was managed by anti-war well-wishers, and not stage-managed by the KGB at all.'

'I've seen that,' said Shirley, whose tutorial had come to an end.

I wondered whether to change the subject, and while doing so, cast a glance around the pub. The G & S memorabilia prints and pictures were everywhere about us, and people were still ordering drinks at the bar. I could not believe that any of them were in the throes of the sort of conversation I was having with Shirley, who was lovely, but steelier in beliefs and resolve than perhaps I could ever be. But did she exaggerate the virtues of the Soviet Union?

'One thing that antagonises a lot of people against the Soviet Union is the refusal to accept dissent and the oppression of political dissidents. I can't stomach that.'

'Neither can I,' said Shirley. 'It desperately needs change, but as long as the Soviet Union is under siege, the more difficult it is to end the siege mentality. But that can't excuse this terrible war against Vietnam.'

'I'm sure you're right about that,' I said lamely, and without the excuse of lameness for not taking part in the big march.

Our glasses empty, we repaired to our respective homes. I decided that the moment was not ripe for inviting Shirley out on a more personal level. Or for investigating her friendship with Bob Hardy.

24

During this first term of teaching I sometimes had to remind myself that the students I shared classrooms with were present not only to provide me with a living and the beginnings of a quiet career, but were real people in their own right, with lives, hopes, anxieties, ambitions or no ambitions, of their own. I was shocked by the assumption of my office-sharing companion Stanley Payne that he could criticise students to their faces without applying the boundaries I felt instinctively to be in place. On one occasion I overheard him telling a male student, in the presence of others, that he was 'a lazy little devil'. He told another young man, who had a swollen and infected lip, that he should keep away from unclean women.

I preferred to address students formally, as Mr. and Miss ('Ms.' was not as yet an optional mode of address). However, I confess that on one occasion, when I saw a student with a very messy set of handwritten notes in front of him, I couldn't resist: 'Did the labrador get your notes away from the cat this morning?' 'Oh Christ!' he said, while his classmates enjoyed his discomfiture. I justified this to myself on the grounds that it was good clean fun, with nothing humiliating about it. But maybe I was just behaving as a variation on Stanley Payne. Thinking about it now, I feel ashamed.

When a bureaucratic blow was struck at the continuance of the full-time basic two year business studies course, I did not need reminding that my students were human beings. The small first year class of this course was vulnerable because, after commencement in September, a couple of students had dropped out and numbers were down to five. My teaching week included four or five hours allocated to this group.

First came reports through the grapevine to me, via two different sources, that the class was faced with closure. A day or two later there was verbal confirmation, provided toothily by David Fawcett in the staff room, that the Chief Education Officer had commanded winding it up. He added:

'My reply is and was a ...' (he made a show of blowing a raspberry).

'Come on David,' said Bob Hardy. He spoke in a glacial tone, and stopped short of completing the exhortation with 'you little shit', though I have a theory that the phrase went through his mind.

Fawcett became more sober and explained: 'I wrote him a letter. I told him where he could stick his decision.'

'What did you really say?' asked Bob with as much patience as he could muster.

'I asked him to re-consider his decision, giving reasons as to why he should do that.'

'I hope the reasons were good ones.'

Almost a month went past, after this, without further developments. The students themselves were given no inkling of what was in store for them. Then, at the end of November, came confirmation of the guillotine decision.

I was present when David Fawcett told the staff group directly concerned. Bob Hardy was furious.

'I'm absolutely disgusted for the students' sake that this diktat has been issued at this stage of the term.'

I could see that if there had been any fight in the body of David Fawcett, something more than readiness to dispatch a token memorandum bleating concern, there was none now, and this reality did not assuage Bob's wrath.

'Any more raspberries from you?' he asked quietly. 'Or is it abject surrender?'

'There's nothing more I can do,' said Fawcett. 'I'm going to tell the students in a few minutes. The best we can offer is for them to join the advanced level general certificate course.'

'Even though the two course programmes and examinations are quite different from each other, and it's ridiculously late anyway to leap from one to the other,' said Bob.

'It's not my fault.'

'You could be robust,' Bob told him. 'Tell Plummer and the Chief Education Officer in bald terms that shutting down the course now, a full third of the way through the year, is unacceptable, as a merger with another course is not a runner, and could give rise to complaints crashing the college's reputation. You could say you will defer notifying the students for 48 hours while the decision is reviewed.'

'It would only prolong the agony,' said Fawcett, tight-lipped.

'For you, yes.'

Fawcett looked miserable for once, and Bob looked at him contemptuously, while saying nothing more. The students were told. They were upset and confused as to what to do. In my next teaching session with them (for a few days' grace was allowed before termination took effect), I expressed sympathy and listened to them. One was the same young man who, not many weeks earlier, had punched caretaker Mr. Patience and then reported him to the police for threatening behaviour, gaining kudos from some of his peers in consequence. With that episode in mind I advised the group not to give the Chief Education Officer a thrashing, and was tempted to add, but didn't, 'and then report him to the police for provocation'. But I did tell them of their right to complain. There may have been complaints, indeed, but I never heard of any, or, for that matter, that the CEO had received a thrashing.

Stanley Payne was more directive than I was. He told the group that in business you need to be able to convert a disadvantage to an advantage, and that was what they had to do.

Bob remained angry about the way this tiny class had been treated, but was still capable of merry-making. At lunch-time, while the students affected were considering their futures, as some of us trooped towards the staff refectory, he held open the rear Town Hall door for Oliver Price, half-bowing and tugging his forelock:

'Again, Bob, again,' said Oliver Price, taking the salute as his due. 'It brings out the squire in me.' I never taxed Price with being a Welshman reinvented as an English gentleman, and imagined that had I done so he would have considered himself complimented. I may, however, have misjudged him.

25

Ann Feldman, having had a certificated fortnight away from work in November, in the final days of that month telephoned in to say she would be back the following Monday. She kept to her word, but that day I was not present to witness her re-appearance, as I no longer had classes on Mondays, and enjoyed a day of prolonged loafing at home in my Holloway Road hideaway. On the Tuesday morning, though, I met Jack O'Neill on the ground level train to Barking after morning fog had helped obscure his presence on the platform. He told me Ann had been in, was more confident, more together, and that things were looking up for her.

'She'd do even better,' he added 'if she didn't get herself entangled with drips.'

As we walked from the station down the High Street to the college, fog was again very prevalent. I was curious to see how Ann was faring. She was not in our niche office base when I called in there, and as I set off on the short corridor expedition to my first class, David Fawcett appeared from the opposite direction.

'Ann just phoned,' he said, large white teeth flashing. 'She said she's not coming in because it's foggy.' He looked at me ironically, then grinned theatrically for at least two seconds. I looked back, surprised. I had not imagined fog to be a justification for absence.

'She did say she might be in later,' he continued. 'I told her the fog hadn't stopped others from coming in.' Fawcett turned on his heel as if to return to his office, and while doing so slid a finger into one of his nostrils.

I proceeded towards my teaching site. At eleven o'clock, as I bore a cup of tea in a plain but colour matching saucer from the trolley in the corridor to the large staff room, while others were doing the same, it was evident that denigrating gossip about Ann was to be had without much asking.

'What will we have next?' Stanley Payne was asking rhetorically, but without lifting his quiet voice. 'I can't come in because the pavements are a bit slippery, or because the sun's too bright, or because the corridor walls have been painted in a colour that does not entirely please me.' This attracted a snigger from two or three who were listening.

Bob Hardy, weighing his words, spoke up in support of Ann:

'I think you should see the announced reason as a symptom of her condition, rather than to take it at face value and dismiss it as deliberate malingering.'

Stanley Payne was not a man to persist against such a put down. He smiled tolerantly.

A short time later I walked into David Fawcett's office when its occupant was speaking unmistakably about Ann over the telephone.

'Yes, because of the fog. You think I should speak to her?'

The answer was obviously yes, to judge from Fawcett's satisfied expression, and presumably he was speaking to Mr. Pringle, who would have been securely out of public view in his office as customary.

Over lunch in the staff refectory, Bob Hardy and I had a table to ourselves. He told me that the liberal studies chief, the hated one, Dai Griffiths, had spoken of Ann's reason for not coming in as 'a paltry excuse' and had suggested she should be shot.

'What did you say to that?'

'I just said this college is full of fascists, and saying that seemed to clear both the air and the room,' said Bob, who seemed, as he spoke to me, reasonably content with the effect he had produced.

'Is there a risk she could be sacked?'

'I think that would be a long, long way down the line,' he replied. 'Places like this move very slowly and anyway the problem for the management is that health is involved.'

I absorbed this, and while doing so, Shirley joined us, followed closely by Jack O'Neill and Oliver Price. Shirley said immediately she was puzzled by an advert she had seen lately. She described it.

'It's an advert for a sparking plug, but on one side of the ad there's a picture of a woman's navel, surrounded by an expanse of tummy.'

Jack O'Neill provided an immediate solution, which no-one present discredited.

'A sparking plug makes a car go. The implication is that it also makes a woman go. The scientific accuracy of that is no doubt debatable, but the idea could be popular amongst male car users.'

Shirley looked unamused, while Oliver Price, with a hearty expression on his face, more farmer squire than ever, declared decisively:

'A dirty mind is a joy for ever.'

Ann never appeared that Tuesday, but she arrived the next day, a day without fog, just before nine. She looked pale, a little lost girl, however voluptuous her body. I told her it was good to see her back, and asked her if she was all right now.

'I got so bored staying at home, so I decided to come in.'

She then immersed herself in preparation for a class. Seated nearby, three quarters of my attention on my own work, I saw her reading lecture notes with attention and betraying visible anxiety. She was moving her face from side to side nervously as she read. Then suddenly she put her hands over her face and ceased movement for a few seconds. Perhaps realising I was there, she removed her hands and looked over at me.

'I'm not cut out for this job,' she said. 'I can't talk.'

She then rose and made for the ladies' cloakroom.

While she was out of the room, and being then alone, without any right or permission to do so, I took the liberty of glancing over the papers on her desk. There was a neat marking plan and a calendar with the days systematically marked off since the beginning of term, ending with the previous day. Her lecture notes were orderly and superbly legible too. Their originator, on the other hand, was an undeniable mess.

Later on that day I asked her how a session with local government clerical officers had gone.

'Terrible, but not the worst I've ever done.'

She had made no mention to me of any concern she might have had about the extra burdens her late absence had given to her colleagues, including me, or about any negative effects produced on the progress made by her students. For Ann the world around her must have looked so grey, even without the addition of London fog, that the inconvenience for others produced by her absences must have been more or less immaterial.

About that time (for he told me about this later), Stanley Payne must have interrogated Ann in his unassuming but intrusive way, and wormed out of her the fact that during her extended absence she had been prescribed drugs by her doctor to deal with her anxiety and depression. She also told him she was living at her parents' home now, that she had finally resolved to return to live with her husband, but that he was no longer interested, having in recent days found someone else. She was not sure what to do now about her Canadian boyfriend.

Stanley told her that his father used to say that there were different ways of looking at a problem. If you looked at it from the problem's point of view, there was no problem.

Ann had listened to this but had said: 'That's stupid, though, looking at a problem from the problem's point of view. Problems don't have a point of view.'

On this issue she had my endorsement. Stanley had also suggested she might try group therapy. He had been, it seemed, making some amends for his previously less sympathetic stance towards her. Responding to this, I asked him to amplify.

'I was thinking that in Ann's specific case group therapy might take the form of sex orgies. Just as well, perhaps, that Ann didn't ask me to amplify.'

'Just as well.'

26

My retreat off the Holloway Road continued to be a place where I spent plenty of unexciting evenings. I had no television. The radio sufficed, my actress landlady's cats paid me frequent and extended visits, and occasionally I had conversations with their owner, but these exchanges were limited by her proneness to self-centred soliloquy. She was not working at that time, but told me she had had a minor part in a pantomime in Norwich the previous year. She went on to say, holding in her arms the eldest of her three cats, a bony creature faintly resembling its mistress:

'The trouble was, I didn't like the accommodation where we were put up, or some of the people.'

She went on, unstoppably vocal:

'We were rather crowded, extra beds crammed into rooms, and there was an eighteen-year-old called Tina. She was a selfish little bitch with a cockney accent. She thought she was something special. She had a boyfriend, and she shared a bed with him downstairs, and that meant the rest of us had less space, as it wouldn't have been right to have more beds in their room. Then one night, another lad showed up, a friend of Tina's boyfriend. He was given a bed in the room next to the one I was sharing, but when I got up in the morning his bed was empty, and Tina's was very full. She was a knowing little madam.'

I felt sympathy for my landlady with regard to the selfishness implicit in the overall sleeping arrangements, but was struck by the fact that my landlady blamed the girl Tina more than her boy-friend. What she was describing was outside my own personal life experience, but I couldn't help asking myself if my landlady was unconsciously disclosing only prudery or, perhaps unconsciously, jealousy of youth as well. She seemed to have no friends outside the cat kingdom.

Unassertively, I suggested to her that all might not have been as she imagined. True, it could be that the girl might have had sex with both men. But unless my landlady knew different, the three-together moment might have been non-sexual, no more than a friendly cuddle-up. She looked at me drily, unconvinced. 'I always think the worst,' she said, putting down the skeletal animal she had been nursing and watching it stalk away without a hint of gratitude. I did not dare to put forward further possible mitigation for the girl: that she may not have consented willingly to whatever occurred, while not wishing to make a public scene.

My landlady, I concluded, might disapprove if I brought Marion – if she was still interested in me – back for the night. Not that my own interest was unhesitating. I had deferred phoning her again after late November.

The neighbours where I lived were of many backgrounds. One afternoon when I was able to return home early from work, an ice cream van with an Italian name on it (and without much business, to judge from the absence of a convergence upon it by children), sailed slowly along the road and paused near my abode, its musical propaganda continuing to advertise its cold and mostly white products. It was then that a man in his forties, and of military demeanour, appeared at a front gate opposite and bellowed:

'English people live here, you know.'

Bob Hardy had told me there were 'a million Enochs' in Britain. I was not inclined to disagree.

27

Early in December I descended from the overland morning train at Barking to find Jack O'Neill already on the platform. He had been a fellow passenger in the next carriage to mine. He looked drained and dazed. He told me he had had a bilious attack the previous night and wasn't feeling well, but didn't want to miss work unless it was unavoidable. He'd only just managed to catch the train at Upper Holloway, having, as he said, ridden his bicycle like billy-ho to the station, then being forced to abandon it in the station yard. I must have been at least some seconds ahead of him when entering the train at our journey's commencement, and had missed viewing his manic arrival just before the train doors closed.

I saw him in the college on and off later that day, less conversational than usual, but surviving his classroom commitments. I gathered from him days later that the bike he had abandoned had absented itself by the time he returned to Upper Holloway. 'It wasn't much of a bike,' he said without regret for the loss. 'It didn't have a saddle,' he added, 'but I was so much in a race to get there, that I didn't need one. It had pedals of a sort.'

The following day things with Jack seemed to have gone from bad to worse. When I talked with him at the mid-morning break in the annexe staff room, his fingers were wandering uneasily over his chin and face. He reached for a paper handkerchief which was already in ribbons.

'You look anxious,' I said.

'I'm not surprised I look anxious. I am anxious. Sally attacked the coloured man upstairs yesterday evening while I was here. She's not been so good at taking medication over the last week or so...'

I gathered that for Sally hospital and a court appearance had been programmed in.

Despite this latest trauma, expressions of sympathy for Jack from his colleagues were soon replaced in the conversation by concentration on a scandalous event which had occurred in the college the previous day. The caretaker – none other than Mr. Patience – had confronted another form of student unruliness. I received a full account from Peter Dawlish, whose daily stationing of his two-seater in the car park had brought him to chatting terms with Mr. Patience. Jack O'Neill was seated next to me as Bow Tie told his story.

Mr. Patience had discovered at lunch-time that a basement room in the main building was locked on the inside. No one had responded to his thumping on the door. He had left the scene to fetch a head of department. More knocking and demands that the door be opened finally caused two students to emerge.

One was thin, bearded, long haired and male; the other was longer-haired, plump, curvy and female. The male was taciturn, the female sheepish, not knowing, so Mr. Patience later asserted, bushy eyebrows raised, where to put her face. Though fully dressed at that moment, there was a supposition they had both been less so not long before. Both Mr. Patience and the department head had been lost for words, immobile, and had stood silently as the couple departed the scene.

Thinking of my landlady, I said: 'You're assuming the worst. They could have been reading *Paradise Lost* together.'

'More likely doing the research for *Paradise Achieved*,' was the alternative assessment offered by Jack O'Neill. His additional observation about the episode was characteristic and Shakespearean: 'Let copulation thrive'.

'Oh, really, Jack,' said Peter Dawlish. 'There's a proper time and a place for everything, and the college basement is not an appropriate venue for casual mid-day sexual relations.'

'Not even for staff?' inquired Jack.

'Not even for staff.'

Jack, however much under the weather from an almost impossible family situation, always seemed to be able to move speedily into recovery mode. His sexual philosophy was further publicised by his theatre visit in mid-December to see the very fashionable musical *Hair*, rich as it was in sexualised dancing and popular music. The following morning his elation in the staff room among a cluster of male colleagues knew no bounds. 'It's practically my programme,' he declared, 'plank for plank. You could lay any bird on earth after taking her to see it.' Then he noticed Shirley looking at him with eyebrows raised.

'I apologise,' he volunteered, still on a plateau of delight.

'I should think so,' she commented without wrath.

As December advanced, a catchy popular song of that year from 'Lulu', a youthful and exuberant female singer – *I'm a Tiger* – heavily reliant on its title for its content, many times heard on my hissing little radio, kept buzzing in my head. Ann Feldman's crises seemed to be receding, and I, for one, was grateful for this. On the whole she continued to get into work; on the whole she continued to stay at work, having arrived. Opportunities for demonization of her had diminished, but I could not have been the only one to have the conviction that Ann was unlikely ever to be suited to teaching in further education, even if her present life-crisis dilemmas were resolved.

When I saw her marking essays for a full time group and,

looking up at me, drawing negative conclusions from their written efforts ('They don't know anything...'), I could not help feeling as much sympathy for Ann's students as I did for her.

She seemed to be indifferent to the fact that college management (notably Pringle and Fawcett) were said to be dissatisfied with her; and to dismiss as of no import the request of David Fawcett made to her to discuss her absences and illness with him. Perhaps Pringle's own relative passivity on the subject had led to inertia on the part of 'that little shit Fawcett', for Ann told me, after she had seen him, that 'he didn't say very much'.

One day, soon after, Ann appeared at college looking different: her hair was up, her dress high-necked and almost staid, though hardly hiding what Jack O'Neill referred to once as 'an intriguing set of curves'. It was the day, I learnt later from Stanley Payne, that she suddenly felt ill in a class, and went out for a walk to recover. He did not need to tell me, a look was sufficient, that he associated the event with menstruation. 'Are you an enthusiast for equal pay for women?' he enquired, without waiting for an answer.

He went on, fixing me with a mildly melodramatic stare, to say he had confronted Ann while sitting alone with her in our shared office. He had told her:

'The trouble with you, Ann, is that you can't say no.'

Stanley's more kindly mood of not long before, a mood in which he had advised Ann to look at her problem from the problem's stand-point, and to consider group therapy, had been cast aside. His remark, which might have generated sudden outrage on her part, though I forbore from reactive criticism, shocked me. Her response was, Stanley told me, to sit further back in her chair, holding her hands out in front of her body, as if in self-defence. He had then said:

'Oh, you thought I meant sexually?'

'Yes, I did.'

'All I meant was that in all situations you don't seem to make a stand for yourself.'

Stanley had, during this conversation with me, yet again had his hand well inside his trousers. Not that I had ever seen hand movement. He saw my eyes looking at the body area involved, and volunteered that he hoped I did not object to where his hand was, adding:

'I joke, but I have an old groin wound. It's like an old friend. I just say hello to it.'

I did not press him further, but doubted that he could have provided Ann with self-evident examples of her not making 'a stand for herself', without corrupting the meaning of the words. It was his quiet, helpful, superficially bedside manner, and his confidence in her continuing willingness to listen without angry riposte, that enabled him to get away with such offensiveness. Ostensible friendliness, underlying denigration.

When Stanley attempted encroachment on the lives of others, he did not always find such a quiescent posture awaiting him. When in a casual and amicable way, he asked Bob Hardy, in my presence, what Bob's teaching hours were, Bob snapped back: 'What right have you got to investigate my hours?' Later Stanley owned up to me that he seemed to rub Bob up the wrong way.

The annexe staff room was where rumours of impending change were spread, and the latest example was that several of our number were to be upgraded from assistant to full lecturer. This implied hundreds of pounds more annually for each promotion, and could not be sneezed at. It was not yet clear who the chosen ones were in this case, but the possibility did not eliminate grumbling over other matters. Peter Dawlish, for one, was stirred into wrath by being asked to do an extra two hours a week of English teaching.

'In the light of what I already have to do on Wednesdays, it's tantamount to slave labour,' he declared, pointing his pipe towards the doorway, as if anyone passing through bore responsibility for the inconvenience to Peter Dawlish. His bow tie, larger than ever, I thought, seemed to look at me angrily.

'It's enough to make you want to be a hippie,' said Jack O'Neill, who had appeared minutes before from the outdoors world, carrying an umbrella which was in an extraordinarily diminished, broken and weather-proof-less state. It reminded me of a half-destroyed lampshade, or even a cabbage with a thick stalk and one barely surviving leaf.

'I have sympathy with hippies,' said Oliver Price. 'After two thousand years of Christianity,' he continued, 'they pick it up and give it a new name.'

Bob Hardy, always on tap to search out and destroy bogus analysis, came in at this point:

'It's not really the principles adumbrated by Jesus Christ,' he said, 'hippies are more influenced by Indian influences, for example in the preference for solitary contemplation.'

Oliver Price continued to pronounce wisdom. 'I would say that Christianity in any event has been the most constructive of all religions.'

'On the other hand,' contributed Bob Hardy in the calmest of fashions, as if putting Oliver's argument on a pair of judicial scales, and as if questioning the weight to be put on it rather than asserting outright that it was rooted in staggering ignorance, 'you can't exempt huge numbers of Christians from complicity in the Nazi concentration camps and the deaths of six million Jews. And that's overlooking what British Christians did in India and Africa.'

This was thrown out in a low key and casual manner,

but Oliver Price had an answer, after a glance at his watch encouraged him to leave the room:

'You're confusing Christianity with Christians, Bob, and not very committed Christians at that.'

Bob, with decency, agreed. He, Jack O'Neill and I were thereupon left to savour a minute or two of stolen class time before we ourselves responded to the call of duty.

The term ended tranquilly for me. For a female member of the department's staff who was leaving, it ended with the customary farewell ceremony. This was my first experience of being a witness at such an occasion. Mr. Pringle presided, having emerged from his refuge of an office ('blinking into the winter sunlight like a mole emerging from his river bank home', according to Bob Hardy), making a rare excursion from the big impersonal building to the more homely, older-generation annexe staff room. I noticed, as I happened at that moment to find myself following Pringle, that he took the short route through the Town Hall, as others, including myself, had continued to do, despite his decree of months previously that staff should circumnavigate that building. 'We must continue to flout his diktat,' Bob Hardy had advised, twinkly eyed. 'We must carry on marching through it like brash conquerors.'

We were all gathered, some twenty or twenty five of us, including the Major and the black Guyanese liberal studies teacher Shirley and I had met at the presentation of *The Sugar Reapers*, and also, of course, the teacher who was departing. This was, Peter Dawlish advised me, a woman with fish eyes and colourless personality who taught on secretarial courses. She was leaving for reasons of advanced pregnancy, and we listened to a perfunctory presentation speech from Pringle. 'Mrs. Dash,' he said 'is leaving for perhaps the nicest reason of all...'

'Here's to the new Dash,' interrupted the Major noisily,

lifting an imaginary glass, while Mrs. Dash went on to say something grateful and unremarkable in response.

During the farewell ritual I exchanged a friendly greeting with Shirley, and asked her what she was doing for Christmas. 'Parents,' she said in a sighing way.

She added, after a moment: 'What are you doing for Christmas?'

'Parents,' I said, in an equally stoical way.

Mr. Pringle left early, presumably anxious to return to the safe obscurity of his den. I was in earshot before he moved off, and heard him say to David Fawcett that a part time teacher was needed the following term for sociology. Bob Hardy, overhearing, contributed that he knew of no queue of candidates.

That evening I telephoned my university friend Alan to tell him of this vacancy. I did not mention Marion to him. He told me he would immediately get off a letter to Pringle, renewing the offer of his services, and at short notice.

During December, despite earlier expectations of a summary end to our liaison, I spent two or three evenings and a night with Marion, without questioning her about her unavailability for a while previously. I had resorted to the telephone once more and she had answered, and without hesitation agreed to meet as if there had been no gap in our meetings. When we met she was as jolly and informative as before. She volunteered nothing more about involvement with other men, and I did not interrogate her.

So we faded away for the Christmas break, which I shall largely bounce over for present purposes. I spent the two special days and even the New Year with my parents at their home in Sussex close to the Surrey border, and recall that the days between Christmas and the New Year greeted me with icy cold and even snow, several inches deep in the kerbsides and gardens. It was luxurious in my parents' warm and centrally heated house, but stifling in other ways, and I was not sorry to return to my own more amenity-free home.

One late evening early in January, before returning to the college for the new term, I was about to retire to bed when through the window I caught sight of the moon. In the darkness it seemed fuller and brighter – a radiant orb of white fire – than remembered, but undeniably thoughts of current space endeavours by the Soviet Union and America had made me more alive to the moon's existence. It was manifestly real, a place as well as an image on the night sky, and a place where, who could doubt it, a spacecraft might make a manned landing some time soon.

28

January 1969. Odysseys into space writ large. A Soviet space endeavour, rivalling American pioneering, was very much in the news. Two spacecraft, orbiting the earth, docked together, and two of the three astronauts in the second arriving ship transferred to the first, while the second craft returned to earth with its sole remaining pilot. I read about this, marvelling and recalling Jack O'Neill's expressed preference for relieving the hungry over cheering on the space explorers.

Both American and Soviet astronauts were surviving risky operations, and on the year's first Saturday morning I was personally jolted into a more intense awareness of how easily human life can be snuffed out. Having visited Muswell Hill with the aid of a London bus, and having bought in a bookshop there a copy of the latest 'Lewis Eliot' novel by the ageing Charles Snow – *The Sleep of Reason* – I returned to the Holloway Road on foot. As I descended the main road from Highgate to Archway, sticking to the right hand pavement, a red car, a Ford Capri, overtook me. It was advancing as it should on the left hand side of the road, not travelling at any boy racer speed. Then came harsh and inexplicable sounds, as if several wooden fruit crates were being smashed in rapid succession, and repeated thudding came next, the whole process occupying no more than two or three seconds. It felt to me as if the thudding emanated from inside the red car's bonnet. The car's brakes had been applied and the vehicle was screeching to a halt. I had kept walking, but moving faster, and was now almost level with the now motionless vehicle.

A man, or the body of a man, suddenly visible, rolled forward from the front of the car. The body was loose, arms and legs moving as if without a directing intelligence. I was now ahead of the accident by a few yards. I turned to look back. Behind the car, scattered on the road the car had passed over, were the remains of a white paper bag of fried chips. The body was dressed in trousers, shirt and pullover. Then it rose to its feet, holding hands to head, making loud moans, inhuman, terrible sounds, and fell down again in the road. The driver of the car had emerged and ran forward, standing over the now prone figure. I stood and watched, numbed and glued to the spot. A woman dashed out from a house on the far side of the road, and halted there for a moment, before running back, of course to phone for an ambulance. The man moved once more, slightly, and was then still. The woman came back from the house and held the man's still hand.

There was nothing I could do to help, other than to hover uncomfortably over a tragic and disturbing scene. I knew nothing of first aid. After crossing the road and speaking to the agitated and upset driver, who reassured me he would wait for the police and the ambulance, I walked on in a half-trance. A few minutes further on an ambulance came past me, surging uphill. Once home I phoned the police and left my details in case I was required as a witness. I never heard anything more.

The Tuesday following, on the last leg of my journey to the college, having ascended to street level from the underground station at East Ham, I caught up Jack O'Neill. He was holding a book in one hand, and was engrossed in reading as he advanced slowly along the High Street. (I soon learned that the cause for his concentration was a volume of poetry by Baudelaire.) As I drew level, crossing a road at a minor junction was called for, and Jack, while breaking away from his book to greet me, simultaneously stepped forward. It was a dangerous thing to do. A large van was close to striking him. Seizing his arm in an instinctive action, I hauled him back. He thanked me, but was also angry. 'That driver was no older than eighteen,' he said. 'The sheer savagery of it. People are obsessed with the power of the machine.'

We crossed the road. Last week, he said, a neighbour had told him that Sally and little Thomas had nearly been killed while madly running across the street where they lived. 'I don't know what I'd do if Thomas was permanently crippled or something.' He continued:

'Love is the biggest thing. I've loved three or four people in my life, and Thomas is one of them. It's not a hoax relationship.'

Most of us, I thought, are less ready to volunteer to new acquaintances confessions of passionate human feelings, and fewer could do so with such succinct eloquence.

About that time I met Alan for a chat, this time, on his suggestion, in *The Macabre*, a formerly much patronised, and now emptier, coffee bar with skull and bone adornments and a juke box. It was just off Wardour Street and could be resorted to, he advised me, as a last refuge after the pubs closed. He was again wearing his beige duffle coat, equipped with peg-fasteners. Inserting a coin into the juke box, I opted for *I'm a Tiger*. I asked Alan, his coat removed, what he knew of the dispute at the London School of Economics, which had soared, as the newspapers were gleefully telling us, into a fortissimo crisis, and what his Professor's attitude to it was.

'He's quite canny. You're referring to the fuss over the steel security gates being put up at various points in the LSE building. The reason of course was to block repeats of last year's occupations of the place by students. You've read about students taking axes to the gates and getting arrested?'

I nodded vaguely, but in truth I had not been active lately in keeping up with all the detail of news.

'Anyway,' he said, after a mouthful of coffee, 'now the School has been closed and the students don't know whether they're coming or going. Professor Schwarzenberger of course – though not directly involved – was all for the gates, but he's careful to ally himself with the majority of the staff.'

'Isn't physically attacking the gates going a bridge – a gate – too far?'

'I think so. A couple of lecturers are facing the sack for supporting that. It's not the kind of battle students can win. At University College, where I'm based, a teach-in on racialism is being organised. That's coming soon. The students are trying to get all lectures cancelled for it. Schwarzenberger's against cancellation of lectures for the teach-in, predictably. He says he was a Marxist as a student once, and he talks about understanding how the moderates have to defer to the radicals, and he talks about students generally as if they were children.'

I thought of the ageing china-doll-faced teacher at East Ham who regarded our own students in a similar way. She had lately told me she had distributed application forms for student exam entries for which the closing date for fees and completed forms was the 24th of that month. 'I've told them,' she had said to me, 'that the closing date is the 17th. That should get the applications in on time.'

That meeting with Alan, addressed briefly in my journal, was not prolonged, and I remember nothing more of it.

I spent an evening, unexpectedly, with Shirley. Meeting me by chance in a college corridor, she had, looking solemn, suggested quite suddenly an excursion with me that same evening to a pub at Clerkenwell Green. We agreed we would meet there. She added that she could do with cheering up. I wondered why. Clerkenwell was a place then unfamiliar to me, and after ascending from Farringdon station, where the underground tracks were wide open to view from above, I walked up the sloping road towards the Green, behind which a white church reached into the sky. High above the far side of the tracks I could see the large corner office of the Communist daily, the *Morning Star*.

Shirley was inside the pub already, and was eyeing up the bar billiards table, on which wooden mushrooms were already positioned for play.

'I think I'm in red territory,' I told her.

'You're right,' she said. 'People from the *Star* drop in here quite frequently.'

The solemn expression on her lovely face which I had seen that morning was still present.

'I asked you to join me,' she said 'thinking you might cheer me up. Sorry about the selfishness. Let's have a game.'

Neither of us had much aptitude, but we set to with a will. Each of us frequently felled wooden mushrooms with clumsy cue work, but the process was exhilarating, and Shirley came out the winner by a fairly narrow margin. I had refrained from asking her why her spirits were down. Now she told me.

'I needed that,' she said. 'A good friend of mine was killed last night. In a stupid kind of accident.'

I was taken up short and said suitable things. Shirley told me about her friend, whom she said had formerly worked at the *Morning Star's* office, and had lately been awarded an Arts Council grant. He was a young writer of acknowledged promise. The previous night he and a group of male friends had gone out drinking together and had landed up late in a night club. There a couple of the group had become rowdy, and all had been ejected from the club, though not aggressively. Shirley's friend had, just inside the outer door, tripped and fallen backwards. He had fractured his skull on the pavement. That was it. He was dead.

'I can't believe it,' said Shirley. 'He was so full of life and now he has none.' Her eyes were filling with tears and she wiped them away. I told her of my own observation, days before, of a probably fatal road accident, and of the near miss involving Jack O'Neill. She then proposed we move to Soho.

Without discussing exactly where we were making for, we walked to the underground station and bought tickets. Soon emerging at Tottenham Court Road, we strolled silently westwards along Oxford Street. Having turned into Wardour Street, passing by *The Macabre,* on Shirley's suggestion we entered a pub called *The Intrepid Fox.* 'I've been here a couple of times with Bob Hardy,' said Shirley. 'The upstairs bar is often half-occupied or empty and you can stretch out and have a conversation.' Up the narrow stairs we went and disposed ourselves in chairs designed for comfort.

We were the only upstairs customers, and this time I bought the drinks. Shirley obviously had the death of her friend weighing heavily on her. I asked if she knew his family.

'No, and I may not meet them. He was out of step politically with his parents. We – I mean the group of us – may not be invited to the funeral.'

'And are your own family in step with you?'

'Very much so, and expectations of me politically have always been relaxed.'

I asked if Bob Hardy had been on the big Vietnam war march, and she said he had been, though with another group somewhere further back in the procession from where she had been. She had not seen him till later. I avoided asking more, and changed subjects, asking her if she read fiction, and telling her I was reading the latest novel by C. P. Snow.

'Oh, *The Sleep of Reason,*' she said. 'I tried to get into it a few weeks ago. The narrator is a near duplicate of Snow himself – a man starting out with obscure Midland town origins and finishing in the academic and political elite with a knighthood. Discreetly claiming much wisdom and insight. Liked by everyone. A complacent old bore. An Establishment man pretending he wasn't.'

'All that doesn't stop Snow from writing a good novel,' I claimed, explaining too that I had only read a few chapters so far, and conscious that I had paid for a new hardback and wanted to get my money's worth.

'No,' said Shirley, 'but the narrator goes on endlessly about successes (the men who rise), and the failures (the men who don't), aggravating women like me probably even more than men. The book's structure is a mess too, and the characters are half-alive. Maybe it needs a change of name: *The Sleep of Talent?*'

This for me was going too far. My opinion of Snow's work was kinder if less well formulated, and I said I was going to read on, and find out for myself. I said it started off dramatically with the threatened sending down of four students for a sex orgy on red brick university premises.

'I remember. But not quite an orgy. There wasn't group sex. Snow wouldn't go as far as to include that. Too prim and proper. His narrator was supposed to be representing the students and, believing he was acting in their best interests, he calmly sold them out. That's my summary, anyway. Maybe I'm being over-critical.'

I asked her what she was reading. She fished out of her bag a colourful if creased paperback by a German author called Stefan Heym, a name unfamiliar to me. It was *The Eyes of Reason*, and I commented on the overlap between the titles of my reading and hers.

'You won't find much overlap in the content, though. It's not a recent book – the hardback was published here in the early '50s. It's about Czechoslovakia immediately after the war's end, with the central focus on a rich but politically divided family,' she told me. 'It has dense life, passion, real characters and real relevance, as well as making the case for a socialist solution. You might find it makes Sententious Snow look tame. I've just got to the end. It probably goes on too long, but still... Would you like to borrow it?'

I looked at the cover, which advertised the book as a *Seven Seas* edition, and Berlin was mentioned somewhere inside as a place of publication.

'East German propaganda publishing?' I asked.

'Certainly.'

'Czechoslovakia,' I said. 'I bet it doesn't say much about any Russian influence.'

'You have a point. But Heym's a real novelist.'

I took it and promised to give it a try. That evening, before we separated at the underground station, I kissed Shirley on the cheek and again said I was sorry about the loss of her friend. What, I continued to ponder, was her relationship with Bob Hardy?

A recent development, much advertised in the newspapers, was that severer penalties had been introduced under new laws for the possession of drugs, from cannabis to cocaine, together with a generous power to police to stop and search anyone they thought might have some. The changes received the hearty endorsement of Oliver Price, who acknowledged he knew little about the subject. 'Do I walk around with my eyes shut?' he asked, when it was put to him during a mid-morning break in the staff room that police might abuse this power, and that the penalties for cannabis possession might be out of kilter with the crime. Michael Hastings took a similar position. 'People are sheep-like,' he pronounced. 'They need rules to follow.'

'Are you included in the generic term people?' Bob Hardy asked him idly.

'Of course I am,' said Hastings.

'So if you weren't subject to rules prohibiting you from murder and rape, you'd soon notch up some achievements of that sort?'

'I think you're taking my point too far,' said Hastings, who stuffed his pipe into his pocket and pointed himself serenely towards a classroom.

I made a small contribution at this point, saying that it was unfortunately true that some police officers abused their powers, and were not above planting cannabis on an innocent victim. Relying on what I had been told by a friend about a mutual acquaintance's recent experience, and using provocative vocabulary but speaking without emphasis – indeed, taking a leaf out of Bob Hardy's book – I said:

'I know someone who's never smoked pot, and who was busted by the police for having it when they had planted it on him in the first place.'

Oliver Price reacted as if I had dropped a fattish slug in his freshly poured coffee, and as if any personal credibility I had previously was now written off. 'Pot? Busted?' he queried. 'You disappoint me. What sort of circles do you move in?'

The discussion flattened out and went on to include talk of the composition of the next government in Britain, a subject on which Jack O'Neill expressed himself less radically than I had expected:

'If you're living in a brothel,' he advised 'it's advisable to have a proper madame running it.' From that I took it that he considered the present Labour government was insufficiently qualified in overseeing – as I imagined Shirley might put it – the cynical and rapacious business of a capitalist society. Later he told me he always voted Labour.

It was at this point that Stanley Payne, who had been keeping quiet, volunteered: 'You know, one of the Fords shop stewards on a course I'm running – he's a bit left wing – said to me this morning that the employers and the politicians are ganging up on the workers.'

Jack O'Neill followed. 'Is there anyone' (he emphasised the word 'anyone') 'who doesn't think that?'

Stanley soaked this up and said nothing. Oliver was not quite so willing to avoid Jack's challenge. 'I like to think,' he said, 'that most of us, including employers and politicians, and even police officers, try to do our best.'

To the surprise of several, I confronted him myself without sophistication. Was I unconsciously guided by recollection of the Major's piano-related antics a few months earlier? 'Where's a bucket?' I enquired, indicating by a simple gesture that an unstoppable upward movement starting somewhere in my stomach was about to occur.

'So,' said Oliver. 'A true iconoclast. And a coarse one at that.'

I shifted to sophistication as smoothly as I could. 'Perhaps, Oliver, your comment wasn't as wise as you might think. The problem is that if you take the line that everyone with authority, power and wealth are doing their best, where do you draw the line to exclude well-known abusers of power such as Hitler, Mussolini, Franco, those in this country who made it their business to appease those dictators, and even that nice Sir Anthony Eden who had a go at subduing Egypt because Egypt wanted its own Canal back? They were doing their best – as leaders that is' – I paused expressively here for a couple of seconds – 'to do their worst. And now we have Labour government support for America in Vietnam.'

I was making up for my non-appearance on the anti-war demonstration of late October. As I completed these words, I had my back to the staff room door, and then felt a hand rest lightly on my arm for a second or two as someone came slowly past me. It was Shirley, who added no words to her supportive gesture.

Oliver Price was now quiet, as was Stanley Payne. 'Well said there,' declared Jack O'Neill, looking at me kindly. 'Even if you didn't mention the little matter of England and its behaviour towards old Ireland. Is our government sucking up to the Unionists or just doing its best?'

There was an awakening realisation that we had bitten into minutes of class contact time and Jack, Stanley, Oliver and I all made a hurried departure, bound for different classrooms. Shirley stayed, and smiled at me as I left.

Oliver Price did not subsequently return to our discussion. Occasionally I was to catch him looking at me, as if weighing me up. Yet I was hardly a menace to his own conformist and colonial-minded perception of the world.

One day, facing a class a few minutes after morning start time, while I was in full flow, explaining some legal principle or other, the door was flung open by Jack O'Neill, who clattered in with an armful of textbooks. From his open-mouthed facial expression, I could see it had been in his mind that mine was the classroom in which at that moment he was allocated to play the teacher's part. Standing in the doorway he said, half-bewildered, but characteristically attending to every syllable: 'I've a feeling this has happened before: clearly there has been a cock-up.'

After this disruption and a guffaw erupting from the students, one of whom queried, as the laughter faded, how Jack O'Neill could ever have got into university, I resumed the teaching task. Jack told me later that day that the civil magistrates' court case against his wife had been adjourned the previous Wednesday, that Sally had taken out a cross-summons against their West Indian neighbour, and that the police had a lot to say about her. Otherwise their domestic life was stable, or relatively so.

Ann Feldman's situation also seemed to have normalised.

She looked cheerful, had been making applications for full lecturer posts in other colleges, and had even secured an interview somewhere. Additionally, a man who was neither her husband nor her Canadian boyfriend had been telephoning and leaving messages for her. His calls, after a short time, however, ceased and nothing further was heard of him.

I gathered from Stanley Payne that he had had the grace not to quiz Ann about this latest male interest, other than to extract from her the information: 'I went out with him once. He was a creep.'

Meanwhile, my friend Alan had been interviewed by Mr. Pringle for some part time teaching in sociology. Alan was given the job on the basis that it was expected to run for a term, possibly to be extended. I heard the result from him by phone the same evening. 'We are now colleagues,' he said. 'I was very reticent during the interview. I didn't mention the class struggle or the exploited proletariat once.'

Armed with this news, I told Bob Hardy, when I next saw him, that a friend of mine had secured the visiting lecturer sociology work. Bob was immediately curious:

'You may not know that I sat in on the interview.'

'I didn't.'

'I don't think Pringle spotted that he was appointing a Marxist. Isn't he one?'

'How did you deduce that?' I asked.

'Well, for one thing, he was clutching a copy of that Tariq Ali paper, *Black Dwarf*. Though Pringle wasn't eagle-eyed enough to have seen that. And even if he had been, he'd have surmised it was a mutual support magazine for black dwarves.' This second thought was expressed with an extra large grin.

'I'm sure you're right.'

'So is he or isn't he a Marxist?' asked Bob. 'I won't gossip.'

'More or less,' I replied, though I considered Alan a playboy as much as a socialist.

★

There came a small earthquake. It was precipitated by the publication in the *Guardian* of a letter from Martin, the German-origin liberal studies teacher who was profoundly out of sympathy with his lazy and illiberal liberal studies chief. I first heard about it early the following week, when Bob Hardy brought in to my office base a torn off sheet from the newspaper, and set it down on my desk. Both Stanley and Ann were elsewhere. The printed letter I read alleged race discrimination against the employers of the college's gas fitting apprentices. (When I wrote up this event in my journal over the next week or so, I was, fortunately, generous with detail about the letter and the affair as a whole.)

Martin's opening words announced that he was a lecturer at East Ham Technical college, which was the main further education centre for gas fitting apprentices of the North Thames Gas Board. He went on to say that although the recruiting area included 'districts of heavy concentrations of immigrants', during the five years he had worked at the college, he had come across virtually no 'coloured gas fitting apprentices'. The only two exceptions were an Anglo-Arab and an Anglo-Indian. Martin stated he had taken up this issue of colour discrimination repeatedly with the Gas Board by letter, but had received no replies whatsoever until he had taken up the matter with his MP. The answer he finally achieved had asserted that no records of the colour of employees were kept, and that racial discrimination was not practised.

After this introduction came Martin's stark conclusion. Either, he wrote, no 'coloured immigrant' was applying, or that all such were failing the 'required test'. Then, the killer sentence: 'A more likely explanation is the one given to me confidentially, that the North Thames Gas Board refuses to employ coloured gas fitters because some customers might

151

refuse them entrance to their homes.' Martin's full name and home address followed.

Having read the letter once, I glanced back through it. The linguistic mannerisms of Martin were much present. There was the use three times of the term 'coloured gas fitting apprentices' and the insistence on avoiding abbreviation of the title 'North Thames Gas Board' after first use, while the term 'heavy concentrations of immigrants' was borrowed, perhaps, from the vocabulary of World War 2 tank battlefields, encouraging the fantasy that the expression was taken from an aerial survey. Pedantically expressed as the letter was, I could hardly quarrel with the submission Martin had made, or deny him respect for making it publicly. His message to the Gas Board amounted to a head-butt in the stomach for the Board's recruitment practice, and a considered call for overdue change. Bob told me Martin was a brave man and had done the right thing, and I agreed with him.

But Martin had, by this whistle-blowing (a concept then not as popular as now), exposed himself to risk as well as exposing the Gas Board for its collusion with racism. Bob told me that Martin had been summoned the previous day to the office of the thin and prim Principal, Mr. Plummer. His carpeting had been, he learned, the direct result of a 'rather fierce' telephone call from a senior manager of the Gas Board, who had asked Plummer whether or not Martin had obtained college management permission to make public his concern. Bob told me of Martin's account of the interchange, which I obtained more fully some days later from Martin himself. The essence of the conversation in the Principal's office was as follows:

Martin: 'I wasn't aware I needed to obtain permission. I was giving away no confidential information. The matter I raised is of public concern.'

Plummer: 'Yet your letter itself says the reason for no coloureds was given to you confidentially. Isn't that a breach of confidence?'

Martin: 'I did not provide any source of that information.'

Plummer: 'Your letter bandies about the name of the College and readers could easily get the impression the College is supporting a racialist practice.'

Martin: 'It ought to be plain to anyone that the College has nothing to do with the Board's recruitment practices.'

Plummer: 'If the Board is concerned that housewives might not open the door to coloured men, with the reputation they have for sexual potency, and bearing in mind what their husbands might say, isn't that for the Board's judgment?'

Martin: 'I have difficulty in believing you said what you have just said.'

Plummer: 'In any event, who amongst us has a perfect record in these matters? Have you entertained – ?' (He named the Department's one black lecturer – the Guyanese teacher who had been, as I have described earlier, in the auditorium at the *Sugar Reapers'* presentation in the Festival Hall.)

Martin: 'That is none of your business.'

Plummer: 'I believe that you are Jewish. Perhaps that makes you ultra-sensitive.'

Martin: 'The problem is not me; it is the barring of admission to gas fitting of coloured immigrants. This is contrary to the expectations of the Race Relations Act now in force.'

Plummer: 'I am thinking more and more that you are not a fit person to teach liberal studies. This matter will be considered further.'

Hearing this account with the help of Martin's authoritative memory, I thought again of my own East Ham interview, when Plummer had preferred me to the young black man who may have been better qualified than I was.

Bob Hardy told me the treatment Martin had received was a scandal comparable in principle to the Dreyfus case, if less likely to gain national publicity, and that Martin had declined Shirley's offer, as the department's trade union representative, of support in the interview. When I saw Martin, I congratulated him on what he had done. He thanked me in an embarrassed way.

Jack O'Neill, on the other hand, spoke to me about the Martin episode in a knockabout, jokier fashion. He too referred to the Dreyfus case. 'J'accuse le North Thames Gas Board,' he suggested (producing a mature French accent), 'would have been a more suitable opening for Martin's letter.' He went on to talk about Che Guevara, the murdered Cuban revolutionary, and proposed fantastically that Guevara had gone to Bolivia to start another revolution because he was upset that the revolution in Cuba had been successful. He added to this that Guevara was the Martin of Bolivia.

'Surely,' I said, 'it's not a joke.'

'All right,' he said. 'Martin did the decent thing, of course. Even if my wife Sally would have withheld her approval.'

I had a discount lunch with Bob Hardy in the local Chinese restaurant, and learnt a little more there. Bob had a lot of time for Martin generally. 'He doesn't have a very easy life,' he said. 'For one thing his wife has had a number of nervous breakdowns and was in hospital only recently. He doesn't talk about it like Jack does. And he does most of the child care when he's not at work. His wife isn't really interested in the children.'

'Did you know he'd been writing letters to the Gas Board,' I asked.

"Martin had mentioned this to me. But I didn't know in advance about the one to the *Guardian*. He's certainly put the noses of the Enochs here out of joint.'

'Has he done things like this before?'

'He does upset people from time to time. Last summer term he got fed up with there never being anything to drink water from in the Town Hall canteen. So he brought in a load of plastic yoghurt cups – all meticulously washed – and left them for the catering manageress with a note.'

'Mrs. Patience?'

'Yes, wife of Mr. Patience the caretaker. She wasn't grateful.'

'Was she patient?' (My conversation, like that of others, could at times lack sparkle.)

'She was bloody furious about the implied criticism, and gave instructions he wasn't to be served next time he came in. But then she relented. She's a kind woman at bottom.'

Hardly pausing, Bob went on. 'Don't you think the state of the canteen is disgusting? Haven't you noticed the dirty plates are never removed?'

'Never?'

'Well, not when they should be. But I'm not going to take it up with Mrs. Patience. She might set her husband on to me. Riding his motor bike. And then I'd have to punch him on the nose and report him to the police for provoking me.' Clearly the tale of the student, the car park and Mr. Patience was not yet deducted from Bob's memory.

A week later, I learnt more of the unwinding of the Gas Board letter saga. By this time Martin had accepted support from Shirley, who was present at a second meeting with the Principal. Plummer was then asked to apologise for his remark associating Martin's being Jewish with motivation for writing the letter.

When Martin gave me his version of this meeting with Plummer, he added: 'The upshot was that the Principal did apologise to me.'

'So how do you feel now?'

'Well, I don't think I shall ever get promotion here. Not that I'm seeking it.'

In the days that followed, discussion in the staff room on the subject continued, when Martin was not present. 'He's a funny devil,' said Stanley Payne to me when we were alone. 'He doesn't speak to me, because he thinks I'm a racialist,' he went on, 'and because I don't hold progressive ideas about crime and punishment.'

'Such as?'

'Well, I'm against capital punishment but I do think convicted prisoners should be beaten in prison to remind them of their crimes. Prison is like a holiday camp for a lot of them. Wouldn't you agree?'

This had been said without heat, though Stanley's eyes had, I decided, become piggish when he said it, and it infuriated me. Without pausing for reflection, I threw back at him, as calmly as I could: 'Presumably, as you have such a down on women, you would have women prisoners beaten harder than the men, especially during the time of the month.'

Realising he had gone too far if he wanted to maintain a good working relationship with me, Stanley retracted swiftly, grinning: 'I was being jocular. Just getting you going.'

'You succeeded.'

'Anyway, Martin is a funny bird.'

At another staff room moment, Oliver Price pronounced that Martin had a persecution complex. Someone else said he was certainly prickly and over-sensitive. Fawcett suggested (speaking, as he usually did, towards the wall or the window rather than to his listeners), that Martin had thrown his chances of advancement away.

In the absence of Bob Hardy and Shirley, I felt obliged to say something in Martin's defence. 'Martin may be funny, prickly, not concerned about his own advancement, and if he has a persecution complex on behalf of others of a different colour, it seems to have been well-founded. So he should be admired for standing up for them.' I smiled into the silence that followed.

Bob Hardy told me later, before being joined by others, that Martin, besides being decidedly ethical, was inclined to be old-fashioned prudish. "If he spoke of sex education, within the 'Boys and Girls' topic in the 'Civic Awareness' course, he would have been disapproving of sexual experimentation before marriage."

'And alongside marriage?'

'Horrified.'

I didn't ask Bob if he were himself experimenting sexually outside marriage, for example with Shirley.

Michael Hastings and Oliver Price, entering the staff room at that moment, sat down near Bob and myself. The small and neat Hastings had heard references to Martin as he came in, and he put in his two pennyworth. He said that if he was selling his house and he had the choice of selling it to a highly educated white man or to a squalid coloured man, he'd choose the former.

'Haven't you dropped yourself in it there?' asked Bob Hardy, as if idly curious. 'What if the choice was between a highly educated coloured man – or even a highly educated coloured woman – and a squalid white man? Why did you put the dilemma the other way round?'

Hastings sucked his pipe, saying nothing, but pulled a face. He had plainly been taken off-guard and felt uncomfortable. I repeated my earlier declaration: 'Surely Martin's making a stand on a question of principle about racialism attracts admiration?' I looked at Oliver Price. He declared, between measured puffs at a cigarette, which I imagined helped to sustain the fruitiness of his voice:

'There are two sorts of people, whatever their colour. There are amiable, pleasant, reasonable people. There are humourless, rigid, immovable people.'

'And to which category does Martin belong?' I asked.

'You are at liberty to surmise,' he said.

'And the Gas Board? Trying to do its best?'

'I'll pass judgment on the Board if and when I have more information,' he said, dodging the question as he departed, calm and undefeated.

But despite the weak staff support for Martin's manner of raising a discrimination issue, I noted that criticism of Martin never, in my presence anyway, extended to criticism for Shirley's unwavering support for him. Some of my colleagues seemed to veer away from risks of being put in their places, however pleasantly, by Shirley.

29

One icy evening, after snow had fallen, I arrived at the appointed time at the front door of the house in Clapham where Marion and her friend Martine shared their gloomy furnished upstairs flat. The place was in darkness. With no-one to answer the bell, I had to cool my already cool heels outside. It was unlike Marion to be late, and I loitered on the pavement in an increasingly disaffected state of mind, hoping she would turn up soon. After twenty minutes she appeared, with an apologetic look and apologetic words.

'I'm sorry,' she said. 'I had to stay late at the office for once.' With that, she unlocked the front door and we went upstairs.

Inside, she was more than welcoming. 'Would you like some coffee or...'

I opted for the 'or' and soon my cold toes became warm together with the rest of me, while Marion herself was as ready for prolonged interactive engagement as I had known her.

At last she made coffee which we drank in bed, while amusing me with her tales of pecking order tensions in her firm, tales of those who crawled and those who were crawled to, tales of command from above and submission from below.

'Yesterday,' she said 'was really funny. My boss Neville...'

'The customer advice department manager?'

'The London Region customer advice department manager to be exact,' she said.

'Yes, go on.'

"He had an invitation to a company 'do' from the managing director. It was very formal. It said:

'A dinner and dance will take place on 1st March at the Russell Hotel for all managerial staff. I should be very pleased if you and your wife would join me on this occasion. Please confirm that you will both be able to attend. Dinner jackets will be worn.'"

'You've got an excellent memory.'

'That's what they all say.'

'So is Neville going?'

"Oh yes, but the no excuses tone of it really irritated him. Then later on there was something else. Neville usually goes prompt at 5.30 unless there's something special on, and the managing director rang me about twenty to six. I said Neville had already gone. 'Gone?' he said. 'But I need him.' He sounded more amazed than angry."

'He had to wait for Neville till this morning, then.'

'Yes, but it put him out. Neville rang him back, first thing as you say, and the managing director seemed OK about it, but still said – well, he didn't exactly say ....'

'Intimated?'

'All right then, intimated, in his gentlemanly way, that Neville was a clock watcher.'

'This is a bit worse than how they are where I work,' I said.

"Later on Neville was having a discussion with someone, and the managing director phoned down. I said that Neville was in a meeting with the chief sales manager. The MD just said 'Interrupt them'. I did, but Neville was really cross, though he kept a respectful front up for the benefit of the MD."

She resumed after a moment's pause. 'Then there was more trouble this afternoon. A customer who'd bought one of our machines phoned up in a rage. He was absolutely puce. Said we'd sold him the wrong type of duplicator. I put him on to Neville.'

'I hope Neville was diplomatic.'

'I don't know about that. Neville's way with customers isn't at its best when he's shouted at. And when it's nearly time to shut up shop. Anyway, the customer demanded to speak to the managing director.'

'And did he?'

'Not then, anyway. Neville told him the managing director wasn't in, but it wasn't true, he was in. So five minutes later the customer phones back. He'd found out from speaking to the MD's secretary that her boss was in, and he wanted to know what Neville had to say about that. He said he was going to make it hot for Neville.'

'So what did Neville do?'

'He was a fool,' said Marion. 'He was standing right by me and scribbled a note of what to say. He told me to say that he was with the managing director at that moment. Which he wasn't, of course. He was with me. Anyway, I told the customer – I'm quite good at telling little lies if I have to – just that. Then the customer slammed the phone down.'

'I don't suppose Neville went home very happy then.'

'No,' she said. 'I had to comfort him. He was quite upset.'

As this story drew to a close I was imagining the nature of the tasks which had kept Marion so late at work. I looked at her, while she flushed.

'So,' I said, shocked but intrusively brave enough to ask squarely: 'Did you have sex with him in the office to comfort him?'

There was a slight pause.

'It just happened,' she said. 'Neville's quite sweet. And it's not as though we're that serious about each other, is it?'

I shook my head involuntarily. I was not used to involvement with women who had such a relaxed attitude to sex. I invited one more answer.

'I get the impression it wasn't the first time.'

'Well, no.......' My inquisitiveness was presumptuous, but Marion saw no need to upbraid me for this, wishing only, without bravado but with growing gaiety, to explain. 'It started at the Christmas party, apart from a bit of snogging before.'

I said nothing, not even making reference to the fact that Neville, as she had just told me, had a wife. Marion went on, with a touch of defiance in her voice.

'I haven't asked you if you've got anyone else. It's not as though you and me are engaged or anything.'

'At least I know where I stand,' I said, with an attempt at dignity, and yet I couldn't help grinning inanely at her.

At that point she kissed me and I kissed her back and made no more fuss. We were still lying in her bed and took advantage of that convenience for a while longer. I didn't dare to ask if she had seen Alan recently. I wouldn't have put it past him or her, knowing what I now knew. What would my landlady say, if I recounted the events of this evening? So I asked myself, during the journey home.

More snow had fallen that evening. Inches of it covered parked cars in the street. I was beginning to fear that I might catch something or had caught it already.

30

Explosion number one of the Easter term had been due to Martin's collision with the Gas Board – and with Mr. Plummer. Explosion number two concerned the Major. He had been having a difficult time.

Trouble had flared in the last days before Christmas, I was told, when the Major had strolled into Mr. Pringle's outer office one afternoon, and discovered that a letter he had days previously put in for typing still awaited attention, left to gather dust in the secretary's tray. The Major was very much lathered up, and had had a shouting match with the secretary, a woman whose emotions were generally almost as close to the surface as were the Major's, and with whom tangling was not generally recommended. In gesticulating, the Major had collided with her elbow, and she had accused him of being drunk.

It was uncontroversial that he had downed several glasses of sherry over a pub lunch. Stanley Payne, who told me about this, said in the Major's defence that he had known him to drive home without a tremor after drinking half a bottle of gin and the same of whisky.

The pre-Christmas incident had been followed, it was said, by a letter to Mr. Pringle from the Major submitting his resignation, if reasonable expectations about typing could not be met. The letter had been passed to the Principal and had sat in his office for weeks before being passed to the Chief Education Officer.

All this Stanley had heard from David Fawcett, who had got it from Mr. Pringle, and the word was, in late January, that the resignation had been accepted, but that the Major himself was not aware that he had actually resigned, whatever the letter said, and did not know he was on the way to the door. The latest news was that he had said in Pringle's outer office, as if the decision to stay or not was still exclusively for him to make: 'I can see I shall have to go'.

This sad story snaked a path around the staff room and, curiously, there seemed to be more expressed sympathy for the Major's plight than had been the case with Martin. Predictably, Bob Hardy and Shirley made supportive noises for the Major who was, when all was said and done, as Shirley said, a teaching colleague.

Stanley Payne went further and, without the Major's knowledge, went to see Pringle and spoke up in the Major's favour. Pringle had apparently said he was sorry, but the matter was out of his hands, and that Plummer was adamant. 'The bastard,' said Stanley to me.

He added: 'The Major doesn't broadcast it, but twenty five years ago, he was in the first waves on the beach on D-Day. He doesn't make a thing of it, but he once told me he has a piece of shrapnel still embedded in his shoulder. Still gives him gyp.'

'From D-Day?'

'From the fighting a few weeks later.'

I felt a sudden growth of respect for the Major, while not making this obvious. But something occurred to me.

'You too?'

Stanley Payne was expressionless, saying only, without emphasis: 'I was at Dunkirk. Later, North Africa. Then Italy. That was where I got my groin wound. It doesn't bother me.'

I took this in, and said only: 'You must think my generation has had it easy.'

'No comment.'

So, the Major was going, whether he actually had intended to resign or not, and that was that.

During these weeks, causes for irritation with Mr. Pringle in the department were on the rise. Whereas Oliver Price, when the subject was raised, would repeat his usual assessment that the man was a gentleman, Stanley Payne insisted that there was a difference between a manager and a clerk. Recent proofs of Pringle's continuing extreme parsimony had emerged. David Fawcett, whose willingness to defer obsequiously to senior managers was matched by an inclination to be indiscreet about them, said that he had been planning visits to schools to attract students, and had asked Pringle if his petrol expenses would be reimbursed. Pringle had said that bus fares only could be paid. Fawcett had thereupon, according to his own account, withdrawn from his proposed mission.

I heard later from Michael Hastings, on the other hand, that Fawcett had gone ahead with his school visits, paying for his own petrol without further protest. 'Put not your trust in the word of little shits like Fawcett,' Bob Hardy advised me, when I shared this report with him.

Such murmuring against Pringle frugality was, however, to take a break. When it was announced, after repeated but imperfect leakages of information, that four of the department's staff on assistant lecturer grades would be elevated to full lecturer status, there was some revival of magnanimity towards college management. Two members of staff who had left or were leaving would now be replaced, despite earlier signals that their posts would be deleted from 'the establishment'. Stanley Payne gave me the explanation that whereas the college had previously had an 'establishment' of about two hundred and ten teachers, this 'establishment' had been slightly reduced, but now was lifted again, under an old formula, by college-wide upgradings. In consequence, departing staff could and would be replaced. The explanation was unfathomable to my mind, but I supposed it to have some factual foundation.

Bob Hardy had told me, with bitterness, that he would not be the subject of promotion to senior lecturer. He had, months before, complained that Fawcett had told him he couldn't be put forward for promotion because he wasn't in charge of a course. Michael Hastings, though, was one of the upgraded staff, and Bob had been enraged, because Hastings wasn't in charge of a course either. This had added to his animosity towards 'prefect' Hastings. He told me that on several occasions Hastings had told the staff room, when Bob was present: 'Ah well, I shall have three hours less on my timetable from next week.'

This was intended to provoke such questions as: 'Why is that?' and Hastings would then have been able to say he was now no longer an assistant lecturer.

The third and biggest explosive incident of the Easter term was yet to come. It was to involve Shirley, but before that, my affair with Marion, if that is what it was, was to enter another phase.

31

Much of February was unappetisingly cold, with no scarcity of wind, and more snow fell. The warmth from my electric fire, which I could move about to increase its influence as much as a short flex and the single wall socket permitted, did not reach far. But it was just about sufficient for my needs and I switched it off at night. I had been brought up to enjoy sleep in cold bedrooms and was warm enough under several blankets; but putting a toe out of bed in the morning guaranteed a shiver. This month was to produce, the radio informed me, the coldest night in the north of England on record. Where I was, close to the centre of London, it couldn't have been as unfriendly.

That month a haunting and sophisticated popular song – *Where do you go to, my lovely* – gently targeted the hedonism of the life of a beautiful, fashion-following, jet-setting, and single young woman who had been born on the wrong side of the tracks, in a wistful presentation that did not altogether exclude suggestions that the target was playing a part, scarred by her origins, and living an empty life. It reached the number one spot in the popularity charts and stayed there. It has stayed in my mind, retrievable from deep down, more so than *I'm a Tiger*, which Marion preferred, ever since. It was played on the radio more than once when I dared bring Marion round to stay the night with me one Friday, having previously told my landlady, less than truthfully, that I had a serious girlfriend and that I thought she would stay overnight sometimes.

'All right then,' said my landlady, without showing approval. 'Can I borrow your two rugs tomorrow, to shampoo them?'

When Marion came round, that Friday evening, we first went out to get some fish and chips, which Marion said she fancied, and a bottle of wine. Back in the flat, Marion was uncritical of my untidiness and of unwashed dishes in the sink, which was tolerant of her. She insisted on washing up while I dried the dishes, and did not complain about the rationed heating.

As usual, she chattered about day to day events at the printing machinery company where she worked. She diverted me with an account of the annual company car allocation. Whereas at the college, managers might be entitled to claim bus fares for necessary travel, in Marion's firm managers could claim personally allocated cars as a straight perk. 'I'm in the wrong line of business,' I said, but without envy.

The regional sales manager, she went on, had acquired the slate-grey Triumph 2000 he had coveted, after phoning round many car show rooms, and her immediate boss, Neville, who had hoped for a Cortina, had been permitted nothing better than a Morris 1300.

At this point I couldn't resist saying that I expected she had seduced him in it already.

'Not yet,' she said laughing. I left the subject.

'Did he get into trouble over the irate customer he was fobbing off and telling lies to?'

'Not really,' she said. "The MD said to him something like: 'If the customer can show we sold him the wrong machine, swap the old one for the new one, will you? This sort of problem should be your pigeon rather than mine.' Neville knows when to change his tune – so he did. And the customer went quiet."

After Marion had gone home cheerily after breakfast the next morning, I did not telephone her until the following

Tuesday or Wednesday, and when I did, her flat mate answered. It was early evening. I reminded her who I was, in case this was necessary. But she said immediately: 'Of course I remember who you are, Clive.' She told me Marion had taken a few days off to stay with her sister in Nottingham.

'She didn't tell me,' I said, but not unduly surprised.

'Why don't you come round,' said Martine. 'You could take me out for a drink.'

This was certainly an invitation I had not anticipated. I was flattered. I hesitated for a moment, but Martine's forwardness got the better of me. I was curious to know why she was inviting me, and about anything she could tell me which I did not know already. So, having no other commitment, I went round to the Clapham flat. From the moment of my arrival Martine was friendly, but composed and not flirtatious.

She was, as I remembered from first meeting her in the Gilbert and Sullivan, more serious in her manner than Marion. That was itself stimulating, and as we found a corner in a grimy windowed Clapham pub, she told me, sipping the cinzano she had asked for, she had ditched secretarial work and was now a croupier at a West End night club, the sort of establishment in which I had never set foot. She was, I thought, preoccupied with her own life, not asking much about mine. I asked about Alan, if she was still in touch with him. 'That,' she said 'went cold after he got stuck into Marion.'

'How did that happen?'

'I probably shouldn't be telling you about this,' she said, solemnly.

'Go on.'

'It was the second night he stayed with me. He got up in the morning to make some tea, and I went to the kitchen to find out why he was so long. Marion was there in her nightie, and he'd just got his trousers on, and they were snogging.

I knew something was going on because I could hear her giggling from my bedroom.'

'Did that finish it between you and Alan?'

'Well, he said sorry, he and Marion were just messing about. But if I hadn't gone into the kitchen then…'

'So did you go out with him again?'

'Once, but it wasn't the same, and I didn't invite him back. When he phoned again after that, he must have spoken to Marion, and then the next thing I knew she was going out with him.'

It occurred to me to ask: 'Was that in November?'

'Possibly.'

'There was one week,' I said, 'in November when I rang a couple of times and no-one answered. After I'd left a message with you.'

Martine reflected before replying. 'Yes. I wasn't around much then, but Marion told me about that. She said the phone rang and rang and she guessed it was you but she felt too embarrassed to answer.'

'She was with Alan then?'

'That was it. It didn't bother her that Alan was just out for himself. She takes life as it comes and leaves jealousy to other people. She's nicer than Alan. He's the superficial one.'

I didn't disagree. Martine and I walked back to the flat, and there was no sense in the air that the coffee we then drank together would lead to anything intimate happening. It had been an evening without real prospect of friendship, though perhaps both of us were in the wrong mood for this. 'Thank you for the drink,' she said.

'Did you invite me round because you were bored, or did you really want my company?'

I asked, not quite able to keep disappointment out of my voice. Martine was reassuring.

'I did think for a minute it might be nice to go out with you, but we haven't really clicked this evening, have we?'

'I suppose not.' Yet, I thought, Martine was more like me in her personality than Marion.

'I've enjoyed the evening with you,' said Martine. Then we kissed goodnight lightly on her doorstep. I liked her, but didn't see her again or, for that matter, phone Marion again, and Marion did not contact me either. So a line beneath was drawn without any farewell. But I did miss Marion, her sense of fun, and her gossip about the people in the place where she worked.

32

The third and largest blow-up of the Easter term was almost ready to arrive. The large staff room in the college annexe was, as was borne in on me ever more palpably, a kind of oral newspaper for facts, rumours and gossip, and that February brought an episode with reverberations greater than those derived from the 'Martin-gate' Gas Board race discrimination cause célèbre of January. But this February episode crowned other, smaller developments, which I shall mention first.

My friend Alan's visits to East Ham had produced no more than a small impact on the department, as he was present on only one day of the week, and during his stay spent almost no time in the staff room. He had, nevertheless, struck up an acquaintance with Bob Hardy, who had briefed him on the classes he was taking, and ensured he had the correct teaching aids.

He had also somehow made himself known to Ann Feldman, who, while now looking generally more upbeat and more alert than she had been, had continued to receive a good quantity of phone calls from a male person who did not usually give his name to others picking up the telephone. This was generally understood to be her former Canadian boyfriend, who now seemed back in partnership with her. Stanley Payne told me that she had carried on one conversation with him ten minutes into her teaching time while her class grew noisy.

Stanley had also noticed the interest taken in Ann by Alan. Knowing nothing of my knowledge of him, Stanley said, without approval: 'He has the look of a young man after the other. However,' he went on, 'I'm not sure she is totally aware of his interest.' He told me too that she had lately turned up without explanation half-way through a two hour morning class. 'A cheek,' he called it. 'She's got as much get-up-and-go in the work place as a stagnant pond.'

I looked at him. 'All right,' he said. 'I'm quoting someone. David Fawcett.' I recall now something that Jack O'Neill said about Ann around that time. 'Lovely as Ann is,' he said (and it was obvious he meant it), 'there is the sense that if a menacing crowd were obviously on the point of rushing her, she would not have much clue that any danger was afoot.'

Ann's interview for a full lecturer post in upmarket west London was now approaching.

I could not, for the life of me, understand why she was pursuing a more senior post in teaching when she was not managing the present one. It looked to me like a plan to escape from one uncomfortable situation to another, in which her inability to meet the expectations of the post would be exposed even more starkly than at East Ham. But even Ann was not certain (echoing her uncertainty in recent times about other aspects of her life), she was doing the right thing in proceeding. She said to me she had almost decided she would not take this post if it were offered to her. Weeks later she was in fact interviewed, but no offer followed. Ann was nonetheless gratified that she was not rejected out of hand. She told me she had been informed at the interview that 'they would like to have her'. I decided not to pass on this tit-bit to Stanley Payne, as it was certain he would give a certain interpretation to these reported words.

She enrolled my assistance, as Valentine's Day approached, in putting the work address of her Canadian boyfriend on an envelope evidently containing a card. She did not wish her own handwriting to disclose the interior content. Her prior research had not gone so far as to produce a full address of the newspaper where he worked, and she asked me what that address would be, as if there was some possibility my general knowledge of central London would provide the missing details. As it was, the name of the newspaper and the umbrella postal district code had to suffice. The street to which the newspaper belonged was left unspecified on the envelope.

Soon after that her boyfriend rang in to the little staff room and I took the call. Ann had a cold, he said, and would not be appearing. Valentine's day had arrived, whether or not he had received her card.

Jack O'Neill's life appeared to be going through an uneventful phase. He himself was never crushed for long. Listening to a conversation between Shirley and Michael Hastings about the immorality and selfishness of professional footballers, in which Shirley spoke disparagingly of a particular football star who had put a girl 'in the family way', Jack, who was simultaneously glaring at a pile of student essays, interjected jovially, addressing Shirley:

'If you don't shut up, I'll put you in the family way.' He followed this with a 'Sorry. It just slipped out'. He picked up an essay and immersed himself in it.

Soon after, he interrupted himself to open a discussion on the topic of the *Goon Show* of 1950s radio fame. The bible of the Goons, he said, was *Ulysses*. This was what the Goons had claimed and what he believed. He connected the comedian Spike Milligan's misfit characteristics to his background – Irish, born in India, the Jew...the Wandering Jew.

He floated on somehow to the subject of investments in unit trusts, after a colleague from another department who had granted himself an extra role as a broker of these investments, had given a kind of informal sales briefing in the staff room. Jack was inclined to invest in some, having inherited money which he regarded as untouchable as income, and was to be dedicated to Thomas's future.

He said, on the other hand, he was convinced unit trusts would collapse in value before long. He explained, laughter coming out of his ears, that he was trying to become middle class; he was the outsider who wanted to join the union, the man who wanted to take up a rightful place amongst those with three bedroomed houses and a car – and who would never make it. He related this to Ben Jonson's play *The Alchemist*, in which everybody was so greedy they were all being gulled. Still, Jack intended to purchase unit trusts.

'I feel like a simpleton entering a brothel-cum-gambling den,' he declared. 'When I get the money back in seven years' time, I'm going to spend it all on whores.'

'I think,' said Shirley reprovingly to him on this occasion, 'that your perceptions of women as existing for the personal use and pleasure of men could be improved upon.'

'I'm hopeless, Shirley,' Jack volunteered amiably.

He showed me the front page of a satirical paper one day. It carried a picture of a small group of northern Irish Protestant clergymen, all of the group except a dominant one having an air of Christian dignity. The hands of one were clasped together. To the dominant clergyman belonged a bubble containing the words: "Right lads: when I say 'Sod the Pope', put the boot in." Jack went on to tell me how the political situation in Northern Ireland was boiling up, with endemic street violence against Catholics by extreme Protestant groups used to preferential rights. He was obviously troubled by the aggression, and by the signs that worse was on the way.

On the train one morning Jack told me of his proneness to be depressed in the mornings, then gradually to pick up, and to be totally ebullient at night. The mornings were difficult, anyhow. Often he left home being pursued down the road by

Sally, Thomas having been left indoors by her. It was then a question of shaking off pursuit before he got on the train. One morning she hit him and he had hit her back. Trying to get away from her that time he had twisted his ankle, and was now limping. His face shining nevertheless, he said to me: 'Limping, it's a metaphor for my life.'

'And do you still worry about Thomas when Sally has him?'

Jack's face became immediately sombre. 'Yes. It will be better when Thomas goes to boarding school. He'll be safer then.'

He went on. His finances were not easy to manage. One day he needed to borrow from me a shilling for the train ticket. Another day, at college, he needed to borrow the price of a lunch. At home, he said, he dumped cash into a drawer, and Sally then proceeded to spend it. And quarrelled with him over it when it was gone. 'I can't go to the theatre or the cinema for a month.'

'Marriage,' Jack concluded 'is a final solution in which each protagonist is bound to seek to eliminate the other.' He said sex in his marriage was a thing of the past, when big rows had generally culminated in a vigorous sexual resolution.

He thought non-possessive women didn't exist in the western world. The answer was to marry a sweet docile woman, to whom man is something large and predatory and disappears at intervals. Jack was, it seemed to me, generalising, as he tended to do, from his own predicament.

His teaching commitments were arranged he told me, so that he had to be on the college precincts for almost forty hours each week. This was considerably more than was true of Peter Dawlish, who was on the same grading level as Jack. It seemed to me greatly unfair that Dawlish had distinctly more privileged conditions of work. Jack, though, while willing to challenge anyone about ideas or books or films, was strongly averse to challenging any arrangement at the college which could put him in conflict with any one. He was not a person to act as an advocate on his own behalf.

In the big staff room later that day, someone mentioned the subject of female students.

This was not a topic about which Jack could remain silent. 'Acres of screwable femininity,' he announced, after struggling for some seconds to articulate the words. Unusually (owing perhaps to his unpopularity among his liberal studies colleagues), Dai Griffiths, who usually confined himself to his own office, was present in the room and spoke up: 'You can't talk about girl students like that. You're a sex maniac.'

Jack laughing replied: 'I certainly am. There is a small, tightly knit group of sexually motivated men in this room, and I am a paid-up member.'

Oliver Price, the respectable, gentleman-like Oliver Price, contributed: "There's a girl in my 'A' Level class who is looking for accommodation. Anyone want to sleep with her?"

Said Jack: 'If she were attractive you'd be sleeping with her yourself. I've noticed people are very generous with what they don't want.'

The discussion was cut short by Shirley: 'You should be utterly ashamed of yourselves, talking like that. Dai is right.' Dai dispatched a glance in Shirley's direction and left the room, saying to those remaining, truthfully or not: 'I've got work to do if you lot haven't.'

So it was that on this occasion right for once was on Dai Griffiths's side. Nevertheless, just after he had gone, Oliver Price, revealing a satiric gift not previously disclosed to me, announced that Griffiths was reviewing subject titles for liberal studies, and that in his own view 'Mayhem in the classroom studies' was one option. He was referring, obliquely, to an incident lately reported by Stanley Payne.

Stanley had described passing along a corridor at a moment when an almighty hubbub of noise was tumbling through the walls of one classroom.

'I opened the door and put my head in, thinking the teacher must be absent.'

'And?'

"Herbert was there. Liberal studies Herbert. He was looking mystified and miserable, standing awkwardly behind his desk. I was going to say something, but then I realised it was the apprentice gas fitters. One of them shouted 'Shut the fucking door in his fucking face', so I thought it sensible to withdraw."

'The student's method of resolving the problem was certainly without grace,' I had put in. 'Did Herbert take command of the situation and shame them instantly into silence?'

"I think he did say something conciliatory, like 'Really gentlemen...', but it didn't cut very much ice, if any."

'So did you just walk away?'

'I went to David Fawcett's room to report it. David was very matter of fact. He said it was liberal studies, and that's how it was. Oh yes, and he said that's what Herbert gets paid for, and that it was a pity there was no danger allowance. Then he laughed like a drain and started picking his nose.'

Fawcett certainly had a large laugh, but his laugh, Bob Hardy told me some time or other, was not on the side of humanity. Bob called it a 'brick shit-house shaker'.

My eyes were opened further about the capacity liberal studies seemed to have for degeneration by the unashamed admissions of one of a pair of teaching colleagues in that sector who were usually together in off duty moments. One of these had vouchsafed to me – a propos of the Major – that he had been responsible for making up a tale that the

Major had vomited not only in the college piano at the end of the summer term, but also in the piano at another college at the close of his previous employment. Until that moment I had believed the story of this earlier event, which had been passed on to me the previous September by the English-teaching trio as a true bill. So it was a lie. The Major had been slandered.

These two liberal studies jokers were involved, I now learned, in a more active stunt than that of circulating amusing but untrue rumours as true. 'Don't spread it around,' the one who had revealed that the Major story was false volunteered to me 'we both get through the week without doing any work whatsoever.' So it was, I reflected, that while Ann's incomplete commitment to her work attracted much odium, these two got away with much more. Such was the value attributed to liberal studies in the college.

Anyway, that afternoon, as I idled in the annexe staff room, this colleague, not much older than I was, brought an engineering apprentice in to use the staff phone. While the student was on the phone, his escort told me with schoolboyish glee that his liberal studies group was spending time and money on the recently commercialised activity of dating through a central computer.

'Are there any females in this class?'

'No girls, but there are a couple of non-whites, unlike the situation with the gas fitters.'

He told me that some of the apprentices had completed dating questionnaires and had sent in fees to a dating agency, and now they had a lot of girls' phone numbers and addresses. So the student using the staff phone was ringing a girl to arrange a rendez-vous with her.

'Another apprentice spoke to some other girl's mum earlier, and she didn't know anything about her daughter doing computer dating,' my colleague said with hilarity.

'But you said you never did any work.'

'Well, today's an exception.'

I asked where computer dating fitted into the liberal studies programme.

"It's Civic Awareness. We're doing 'Boys and Girls' or more exactly, the boys are doing the girls.'" My colleague slapped his knee at his own witticism.

Martin had previously spoken to me of liberal studies being sometimes viewed as complementary and sometimes as contrasting. A computer dating enterprise, it appeared, could be treated as falling within both definitions, but this was hardly a point I could have taken up with Martin, who would have been upset by the misuse of educational time and by the possibility of what he would call 'promiscuity' as an outcome.

To the best of my knowledge none of this episode got back to Fawcett, and if it did not get back to Fawcett, it was unlikely to have got back to Mr. Pringle. Pringle would surely have been concerned about the implications for the college telephone bill, if nothing else.

I now reach the big February explosion. This was another liberal studies-related college development, and this one did involve college management, and with unusual raising of temperatures and sharpening of tensions. It started innocuously enough with a decision by Shirley to invite a speaker to an adult course she ran. The speaker's name was Ron Bailey and the subject was to be 'the squatters' movement'. Bailey was well-known in the press as a spokesman and organiser of a group of homeless people in east London who were taking up quarters in unoccupied homes without any prior agreement as to paying rent.

I heard of this speaker event following attendance at my first college teachers' union branch meeting. Bob Hardy had told me the branch's officers and too many of the members were overly parochial in outlook, acting more like fussy churchwardens than trade unionists. 'If they were churchwardens, they'd be aghast if buttons were dropped into the collection plate, but wouldn't be much interested if a large advance party of Martians landed next to the churchyard, and not actually in it,' he elaborated.

Because of this parochialism, he went on, Employment Minister Barbara Castle's intention to criminalise unofficial strike action had not had a branch meeting airing yet, even though her White Paper – *In Place of Strife* – would itself provoke unofficial strike action. Bob called it 'a strife generator', and said that Castle's recent appearance in a red dress did not hide her betrayal of trade unionism.

At the union branch meeting, the topic up for debate was the slighter one of the proposed reduction of the lunch hour for the engineering department from one hour to forty five minutes. Jack O'Neill attended with me, encouraged by Shirley, I suspected, rather than out of any solid devotion to the cause. He put forward the argument, in discussion with whoever could overhear, during a lull in the proceedings, that the only justification for the existence of engineers was that they could create a world fit for dolly birds to live in.

When Jack came out with this, he perceived that Shirley, sitting a few seats away, had heard him, and he called out to her that he did not mean it. Soon after, she re-seated herself next to him. He then said, admiringly: 'You are the most decorative trade unionist I have ever met.'

She sighed: 'You are incorrigible, Jack.' She then told us about the talk Ron Bailey would be giving next day, when I had a full teaching timetable and would be unable to attend. I knew nothing more until the day after that.

I was early to arrive that morning at the college and, as on so many other occasions, decided to pause at the café across the road before facing up to the prospect of work. Oliver Price and

Peter Dawlish were already deep in coffee and conversation. I joined them. I was then included in the discussion, which after a few minutes turned to the subject of the previous day's presentation by the local squatters' leader.

'Maybe you haven't heard about Shirley,' said Peter Dawlish.

'I don't think I have.'

'She may have spoilt her chances of promotion.'

'Oh.'

'Did you know she was getting some squatters' person to speak about his campaigns?' asked Oliver.

'In general terms, yes.' I said. 'Is there a problem?'

Oliver Price seemed unprepared for my having advance knowledge. 'Well, I didn't know about it. More to the point, though, neither did Fawcett or Pringle. I think they're quite put out. Especially Fawcett.'

'This was about yesterday's talk?' I queried.

So it had been, but at that point I had to quit the breakfast arena and take up my duties.

It was not till lunch time that I found Shirley in the Town Hall eatery, and took up a seat opposite her on the same table. No-one else was in earshot. She looked demure enough. And lovely, I thought.

'Have you read *The Eyes of Reason* yet?' she asked.

Although I had done so, I spoke of the Charles Snow book instead. 'Every time I tried to read it, I nodded off.' This was an exaggeration, but I had become dissatisfied, feeling that much of it – built around the trial for the premeditated murder of a child by two lesbian women – was plodding and over-factual. I gather Mr. Ron Bailey came to speak as planned yesterday.'

'Yes, but the talk didn't end as it was supposed to. David Fawcett came in, worked up, interrupting, and it ended with tempers being lost.' Shirley looked remarkably at ease.

'So what happened exactly?'

She told me in sober language. Shirley had introduced Ron Bailey to the full room as a campaigner for more council housing, and as a supporter of squatting in empty properties. She went on to give me a vivid enough account. Physically unimpressive, and with a brown and wispy beard, Ron Bailey had not been bereft of words or of conviction, and had used his time to good effect. He had spoken of desperate need, of large families evicted from council accommodation, being unable in some cases to pay their rent. He spoke of local and central government as having other priorities than building low rent housing.

Towards the end of his talk, without prior warning or request to Shirley, David Fawcett had entered the room, saying nothing and had taken a seat at the back. He listened for a minute, picked up something the speaker was saying about council houses being demolished, and the sites being used for multi-storey car park development, and had intervened with bizarre questions and argument. Somehow he had got it into his head that Ron Bailey wished his squatters' army to declare war on car parks. Fawcett became rude and offensive. He was talking loudly as if to himself, saying: 'He's mad, he's mad. He wants to abolish car parks.'

Bailey had wound up, saying he didn't have time to unravel the confusions of the person who had come in late. No-one, least of all Fawcett, had told him the latecomer was Deputy Head of Department.

'I don't know if you know,' said Shirley, 'but Ron Bailey has applied for a liberal studies teaching post here. Interviews are due in two or three weeks.'

'Is he still on for that?' I asked.

'I don't think so. He told Fawcett he could stuff the job. But that was at the end.'

'So what happened in between?'

'Ron and I went back to the staff room. Ron wanted to make a phone call to the BBC about a chat programme he was going to be on that night, and I showed him the staff phone. Then Fawcett came in when Ron was on the phone, and told him while he was in mid-flow that he wasn't supposed to use it. Fawcett was in a worked-up state, but he must have decided he'd better back off, and he went back to his room.'

'And then?'

"Ron finished his call and asked me where Fawcett's room was. Come to think of it, his exact words were: 'Where does that little bastard hang out?' So I showed him where, and Ron marched down there. The door was open, as usual, and I could see Ron standing in the doorway. Fawcett greeted Ron amiably at first, making some remark that he hoped the squatters weren't going to squat in his room. Ron then told him:

'I don't want to talk to you about squatters. I want to talk to you about manners. There's one thing you haven't learnt and that's manners. That means you don't go around interrupting people when they are on the phone.' Fawcett answered that outsiders weren't allowed to use the staff phone.

'Maybe,' said Ron, 'but polite people wait till the call's finished. You're not a polite person, are you?'

So Ron then took a shilling out of his pocket and plonked it on Fawcett's desk. 'There you are.' Fawcett told him he didn't want it. It was the local authority's phone. 'No,' Ron said. 'It's your big day. You keep it. And you can stuff the job I've put in for.' Then he went."

'But what about you?' I asked. 'Are you in the doghouse?'

Shirley was less ruffled than I would have been in her situation. 'I don't know about that. The funny thing is that Fawcett hasn't asked to see me about it. I've not been told I should have got special permission to ask Ron Bailey to speak. If he tells me that, I'll say that I hadn't appreciated it would cause a problem. We have had other visiting speakers too, and I haven't had to ask permission for them to come.'

'I suppose you've got some additional protection from the fact that Fawcett behaved so badly himself.'

'I think he couldn't bear the thought of the ideas Ron was expressing. They don't fit his conception of what's right and proper. For him a red line was being crossed. A very red line.'

I asked if colleagues had been supportive of her. It seemed they had not, other than Bob Hardy. Hastings, she said, who had asked her if students of his could attend the Ron Bailey event, had later pretended to Fawcett that he wasn't aware his students had been present until after the talk had finished. He was scared of being guilty of something by association with Shirley. Another teacher who had released students in advance to hear Ron then claimed she knew nothing about their whereabouts. She was scared too.

Over the next week or two, the subject of the Ron Bailey talk kept surfacing and re-surfacing in the staff room and the Town Hall cafeteria. One of my colleagues, a man usually possessed of few words, said fairly that it had all got out of proportion, that they had had various political speakers in the past, including speakers from the Communist Party. He expressed the opinion that it wasn't just the fact Shirley had invited Ron Bailey that had got up Fawcett's nose, but that Shirley was known to Fawcett as having left wing views herself. The combination had blown his mind. Peter Dawlish was heard, on the other hand, to express the thought that Shirley had been 'cunning' in not seeking permission for the talk to proceed. 'It'll leave a black mark against her in Pringle's mind.'

An exchange on the subject took place between Bob Hardy and his detested staff room foe Michael Hastings, and I was silently present for this, while engaged in completing a municipal accountants' course register for 'Mr. Register', taking pains to do it properly.

Hastings was sitting, pipe clamped to his teeth, his eyes in a book about the history of sea warfare. Bob brought up the subject of the college management reaction to the Ron Bailey event.

'Of course,' he said, in a philosophical manner, 'all this is bound to happen as soon as someone prods the sacred cow of private property.'

Hastings was immediately knocked by this out of his sea warfare studies. 'I'd bash anybody on the head who tried to take up abode in my house.'

'How much did you say it's worth?' asked Bob. Hastings opened his mouth to reply and then thought better of doing so. He had cottoned on that he was being ridiculed.

'Hm,' he said, returning to a chapter about the derring-do of Lord Nelson and Co.

David Fawcett, in the days that followed, was heard to express the opinion that council houses should be abolished, and asked various staff members in fake jovial fashion, including me, to declare whether they were reactionaries or revolutionaries. I stood my ground when challenged by him, insisting I was neither, or possibly both.

Mr. Pringle did ask to see Shirley, but as she reported back later, he was sweet and said he could understand unused council houses being taken over by squatters. It was a waste they weren't being used. His frugal, bookkeeping mind, functioning in alliance with Christian beliefs, was working in Shirley's favour.

There were no overt disciplinary consequences, as it turned out, for Shirley's provocative invitation to a radical speaker for her liberal studies class. All that happened was that she was told by Fawcett, and later by Pringle in a short letter, that attendance of visiting speakers in future required advance permission from the Head of Department, for reasons of college security. A notice on similar lines, signed by the Principal, was soon afterwards posted on all Department notice boards, though many staff in other departments may never have known of the upheaval in Business and General Studies which had precipitated the notice.

When I saw it, I speculated as to what would have been the outcome had I informed Fawcett or Pringle that liberal studies staff had been encouraging their male students during classes to use the staff room phone to make blind dates with girls. Would Fawcett have uttered one of his 'brick shit house shaker' laughs and treated the misdemeanour as a 'boys will be boys' occasion? Would another bland notice, this time headed 'Use of Staff Room Telephone by Students for Computer Dating Purposes', have ensued?

I was suspicious that a visit by Mr. Pringle to the annexe staff room around the time the 'Visiting Speakers' notice appeared was intended to calm waters troubled by the Ron Bailey affair, though Pringle did not say so. His appearance was at mid-morning break. 'How did he get away from his minders?' wondered Bob Hardy, scorn plain in his voice. 'I'll bet they're scouring the corridors for him. He's probably come over to admire at first hand the sheer intellectual buzz of this staff room.'

'Show some sympathy,' I urged. 'This must be torture for Pringle. He's here out of Christian duty, no mistake about that.'

The bald and benign Pringle made no attempt to deliver a speech. He went over to Michael Hastings, first, regarding him rightly as an ally he could count upon in the daily struggle against anarchism, chaos, over-spending and waste. Hastings, still glowing from his recent grading uplift, was deferentially welcoming, and showed this by smiles and by one or two extra puffs of his pipe.

Bob was another one cornered by Pringle who said, ornamenting his words with his gap-toothed smile: 'Aren't you the one who puts his feet on the desk during classes?' Bob told me subsequently that he had at first passed this off with a shrug, noting mentally that this was evidence of another example of trivial sneakery by Fawcett, who had seen him with his feet so displayed, and had made some snide remark about it at the time.

Bob had gone on to tell Pringle, however, in a sudden rush of malice, pretending seriousness, that there was a colleague who not only put his feet on the desk but smoked his pipe simultaneously, with the effect that students could see the feet of the speaker but not necessarily the speaker's head, which was sometimes obscured by plumes of smoke. Pringle had not responded to this arcane reference to Hastings, and had escaped from the information with a puzzled look on his circular, child-like countenance. Soon afterwards, his innocent smile was back and he departed, his duty performed, enabling him to retreat to his hiding place in the big building.

That lunch-time I had another tête-à-tête Chinese lunch with Bob. But this time, after updating me about his exchange with Pringle that morning, his conversation dried up.

He looked pre-occupied. I brought up the pleasant evening I had spent with him and his wife Diane the previous term, and he became still more silent. I asked him how Diane was.

'Fine,' he said shortly, 'but Diane and I are not getting on very well at the moment.'

I did not press him on the subject, and switched to the matter of the Ron Bailey affair.

I remarked on Shirley's courage in organising the event and in holding firm when the deluge of criticism broke against her. Bob responded with a wide grin and said simply that Shirley was splendid in every respect. Jealousy in me welled up, aware as I was that Bob knew her much better than I did. I left the topic of Shirley, and the meal ended with the smallest of small talk.

The last of Ron Bailey and his squatter families, who were centred on nearby Ilford, had not been heard. The local council, perhaps to the applause of David Fawcett, struck at the movement a few weeks after Bailey's talk at the college by making empty council properties unusable, unsquattable – smashing windows, ripping out staircases and tearing up floorboards.

But soon afterwards homeless families led by Bailey occupied other empty accommodation and the council, for the time being, at least, changed tack and became less confrontational. An offer was made to other London councils of empty Ilford houses at a nominal rent for the purpose of housing their homeless families.

'This,' Bailey was reported by the press as saying, 'is a tremendous victory. We shall be moving into areas outside Ilford to try to force the hands of other councils.' Purely for the purpose of making mischief, Bob Hardy told me he had shown a news cutting with this information to David Fawcett, saying as he did so: 'Looks as though Ron Bailey and the squatters are going great guns.'

Fawcett had replied, said Bob: 'Pity the guns are not being turned on Ron Bailey and his supporters,' at which Bob – well aware of Fawcett's church-going – said that he supposed that must be the Christian thing to do. Fawcett had not produced one of his great false laughs. Nor had he shown any trace of contrition.

33

I must admit now that I have been holding something back, something which has a large bearing on the way this narrative steers towards a conclusion. I have been writing about events in February, but during January, my fifth month at East Ham, I had an interview at a college in the east Suffolk town of Ipswich, for a better paid lecturer position. Not only that, I had been offered the post and had accepted. I was, to borrow the metaphor Bob Hardy had once employed, making good my escape from a prison-of-war camp. Soon I would be under the wire and on my way to another.

After seeing the job advertised, I had applied on impulse, not at all expecting to be rewarded. I had been influenced in part by a growing conviction that my 'large salary' at East Ham was not so large after all. A higher status meant several hundreds of pounds a year more than I was receiving. I had not told any of my colleagues that I had applied, and the interview had taken place, conveniently, on a Monday, my day excused from teaching. The train had taken me early in the morning from Liverpool Street to Ipswich in an hour and three quarters, and during the journey I made a start on reading the book Shirley had recommended – Heym's *The Eyes of Reason*. I found it gripping from the outset. The realities of life for Czechoslovakia and its people – just after the war closed its killing gates – were imposed on the reader immediately.

Once in Ipswich, the novel much in my thoughts, I walked around the town centre for a lengthy period, killing time, and also killing curiosity about a town previously unknown to me, before arriving at the multi-coloured frontage of the Civic College.

In comparison with London experience the Ipswich streets were as devoid of pedestrians as if it were Sunday – in those days shops everywhere were mostly closed on Sundays – but, not quite in the centre, I discovered a small shop dedicated to the sale of publications promoting the theory and practice of anarchism. This retail enterprise had perhaps been smuggled into, and imposed upon, this unsuspecting country town by subversives from some huge and alien city – unless it was conceivable that Suffolk had its own little band of home-grown political malcontents. A card in the window spoke with candour: 'The management does not necessarily agree with all views expressed in literature on sale here.' The word 'necessarily' was underlined twice. My discovery of this shop, and of the cautiously qualified support of its proprietors for the products it dispensed, put me in a buoyant frame of mind.

The college itself was on a more spacious plan than at East Ham, and there were twice as many lifts in the main building. One of these took me up to the sixth floor, and the Head of Department's outer office carried the words: 'Please enter'.

An obvious thought was that at East Ham a preferred sign might be 'Please re-consider your wish to enter and leave Mr. Pringle in peace instead'. I entered, and the friendly secretary showed me to a room where I was to wait. Before long the second candidate joined me. I was later told that there had been a third invited candidate who had failed to appear.

Soon we were invited in turn (me first) to an informal 'interview', where I sat across from the Department Head, a little man with a small moustache, a Yorkshire accent and a business-like manner. Flanking him were the current two law teachers, one of whom was departing, leaving space for a successor. This interview was not a daunting exercise. The

Department head did most of the talking, but the atmosphere was amiable.

The real interview was to be in the afternoon, and was to be led by the Principal, with the Department Head on one side, and a pipe-smoking assistant education officer on the other. By the time I reached this stage of the process, I was feeling nervous but composed. My rival, a young man from some northern city, teaching in a similar institution to East Ham College, had been very voluble, and had in conversation with me expressed dedication to his students and even emotion in their cause. He had gained his law degree at the London School of Economics. I had lunch with him and the departing teacher, who was able to confirm to me, when I asked, referring to the talents of my predecessor at East Ham, the man in a hurry, that he himself did not, whether regularly or on special occasions, mimic either Prime Ministers or Max Miller.

I was first into the serious interview. The Principal was very different from Plummer. Crisply suited, silver-tongued and assured, he bore all the signs in his speech of a man well-schooled in public relations. The investigative process was less nominal than that at East Ham the previous summer. After a number of specific questions, some of them quite probing, I was asked a 'sell yourself generally' question. This was the one question for which I had an answer ready and waiting. Finally I was asked if I was willing to commence a part time teacher training course, and I confirmed (though a voice inside me said that I could always back out of it later), that I was.

The interview done, I did not assume I had been successful. I felt limp. My rival went in and was there for a good half an hour. It was then suggested to us both that we have a cup of tea in the cafeteria and return in fifteen minutes.

This we did. I was on tenterhooks. I then learnt that my vocal rival, who had become even more talkative than earlier, had been actively involved in radical politics at the LSE. He told me of having been arrested twice at peace demonstrations, and as having on one of these occasions spent a night in a police cell. He expressed relief he was no longer a student, saying life was much more peaceful for him now. I avoided both praise and condemnation, and asked if he had ever met Professor Georg Schwarzenberger.

'That fascist? No.'

Back at the Principal's outer office, we sat and waited for another ten minutes. Then the door opened and I was the one called in. 'Congratulations,' muttered my rival.

I was offered the post then and there. Said the Principal in his smooth way: 'It didn't take us long to decide, but we thought you should have time to drink your tea and we should have time to drink ours.'

I smiled in answer, but did not think smiles. I would have preferred speedier progress. I confirmed I accepted the offer of the post, and left the room.

Time then slowed down. My ex-rival was still present, and we both completed claim forms for expenses. He asked me, as we were sitting together, if I had been asked about willingness to do teacher training. I told him I had been asked. He said he had replied that he hadn't agreed with teacher training, that it was a total waste of time.

'I'm surprised you didn't get it,' I said, not altogether honestly. 'You went to a more highly rated university than I did.' 'I'm not sure that entered into it,' he said. However, I was wrong about that, it transpired.

He strode off smartly to catch his train, and then I got into conversation with the teacher whom I was to replace, who told me he had spoken to the department head about the interviews.

'Give me some inside information on the quiet,' I asked. 'Why didn't the other chap get the job? He was better qualified than I am.' 'I'd better not say much,' he replied. 'But the LSE background didn't help.'

He went on, however, to tell me more. During his interview my rival had volunteered he'd been heavily involved in student politics. They asked him if that had interfered with his studies, and he said that being an active socialist didn't interfere with anything. He was jabbing with his finger when he made points. 'The Principal did tell him that politics wouldn't enter into the decision, but you can believe that if you want to. The head of department said to me that the London School of Economics wasn't much of a launching pad.'

Just as well, I thought, as I travelled back to London, that I hadn't, during my own interview, in a confessional rush, spilled the beans about my friendship with Shirley, who 'helped out' at Communist Party headquarters, approved of the Soviet Union save for issues of freedom of expression and its practice of intervening militarily to prop up satellite regimes, who had supplied Tariq Ali with bodyguards for the previous October's massive anti-Vietnam war demonstration, and who had lent me a novel by a flagrantly communist East German author which I could not put down.

34

Now I had guaranteed employment elsewhere, I felt less need to defer to my seniors at East Ham. "I can now say 'Piss off Pringle' if I feel like it," I announced to Jack O'Neill.

"That's hardly impressive. If you said 'Piss off Plummer', on the other hand, that might reverberate throughout your career."

Some three weeks after the Ron Bailey affair, a discussion broke out over lunch in the canteen between Shirley and Oliver Price about 'colour prejudice'. What prompted it was Shirley's having seen, on Jack O'Neill's recommendation, the West End musical *Hair* the previous evening. She had been captivated and mentioned in passing one of its songs – *White Boys Are So Pretty*. She didn't mention – I was to learn this later – that she had seen the show with Bob Hardy.

The conversation might have become inconsequential, but Oliver Price made sure it didn't by his own intervention.

I was seated in the next chair to him while Shirley was opposite, with a silent Stanley Payne beside her. What might have been a series of exchanges in which we all participated became a focused tennis match between Oliver Price and Shirley; a match in which Shirley's service sometimes brooked no return. Bob Hardy's absence was probably a blessing from that point of view, I thought. More of a lateral thinker than Shirley, and driven sometimes (as the reader may have noticed) to making provocative remarks, it was quite likely he might say something which would enable

Oliver Price to wriggle off a hook put in place by Shirley in her deliberate way.

Price jumped in with both feet, but this image hardly harmonises with his leisurely and urbane manner of contribution. What he said, however, certainly set out his stall on the subject to be debated.

'I don't like the theme and title of the song very much,' he said. 'It turns colour into an issue, and it shouldn't be. The race relations legislation that's been passed does the same thing, and it ought to be repealed. It only encourages prejudice, it doesn't stop it.'

Shirley was composed. 'But it isn't a question of colour alone. Colour also denotes a background, doesn't it, Oliver?' She went on: 'A coloured person living here has usually been born abroad, or the parents were born abroad, and mostly in a third world country, such as the Caribbean islands or India or Pakistan. The food is different, life experience is different, religion is often different. Even if Christian, the family culture is different.'

'Yes,' said Oliver Price, perhaps not appreciating fully what he was getting into. He added: 'And probably worse than ours.'

Shirley, who had paused to eat for a moment, did not seem short of ammunition to continue.

'So you're not now actually claiming darker skin colour should be viewed as if in a vacuum, divorced from everything else, are you, Oliver, despite what you said earlier that colour shouldn't be an issue. If you think about it, it is an issue because you can't separate it from the probably different life experience and culture of people who have darker skin colour; cultures you apparently feel dismissive about for some reason.'

Oliver Price, if on the defensive, did not show signs of it in his demeanour. 'I wasn't condemning other cultures at all. I champion ours, because I think it's as good a culture as a culture gets.'

'So what do you mean by culture, Oliver?' asked Shirley.

'You know what I mean by it, and I know what I mean by it.' This was the best he could do. There was no sign that he sensed he might be on the back foot, still less on the point of being pushed backwards over the cliff edge.

"Well, just consider what 'our' culture consists of. Surely it includes a sense of our history and assumptions and prejudices arising from that history. These unfortunately include a well-inset belief in superiority over others. 'The wogs begin at Calais' might be a joke, but it's also symptomatic of the assumption that the natives of our empire, now our mostly lost empire, are a long step beneath us."

'Was the empire such a bad thing?' asked Oliver. 'Didn't it provide orderly rule to high standards.'

'I don't know what history books you've read about the British empire. It wasn't the white man's burden, it was the coloured people's burden. That empire grew through slavery, and the brutal methods of control that went with it. The empire took economic advantage of its subject peoples, made profits from them and was maintained through many acts of ruthless suppression. That's the historical background to issues of race and colour, isn't it?'

Oliver Price had finished his main 'steak pie plus' course, while Shirley's plate had hardly been touched. He did not acknowledge defeat, but edged towards the position that the argument was not an argument which he was losing but a stimulating debate in which everyone was a winner.

'I don't deny the negatives of course,' he said. 'But you mustn't deny the positives either.'

Shirley was not quite finished, and still calm and reasonable in manner. 'Suppose you'd been born in Jamaica, a descendant of slaves brought over from Africa in harsh conditions, would you have as good an opinion of the empire responsible, and of its culture, as if you'd been born here, a white person, with a history of benefit to white people from the empire?'

'I probably wouldn't, though many West Indians seem more than happy to come here. I fully accept that racial discrimination is a bad thing. But immigrants should accept that the majority culture is different from theirs in some ways, and that they should work at integration with the rest of us. Taking people to court at a sensitive time like this is not going to change that. It will only fuel prejudice.'

Did Shirley's short seminar in empire studies have any traction with Oliver at all?

I cut in here, having actually read the legislation. 'It's worth mentioning that the Race Relations Act isn't what it's cracked up to be. It needs beefing up if it's going to deter. It's got practically no teeth.'

Shirley acknowledged this with a glance, but didn't allow it to divert her from attention to Oliver, who was now showing signs of knowing he was under siege. 'But discrimination is real, isn't it, Oliver? The example of the North Thames Gas Board that Martin highlighted is hardly unique. Are we going to assume contentedly that white people can carry on treating immigrants as if they are inferior for ever? Are we going to challenge discrimination by pretending that colour and the Gas Board's attitude to it don't exist? That gives discrimination a green light to continue.'

'At which point,' said Price, 'I'm going to have fruit tart and custard. I'll think about what you've said, Shirley. Maybe I should attend one of your liberal studies classes.'

After he and the silent throughout Stanley Payne had gone, I told Shirley that she deserved a medal for what she had said, and how she had said it. 'It was, I fear, water off a Powellite duck's back,' she responded.

'Does Jack O'Neill know of your political affiliation?' I asked out of curiosity.

'Of course he does,' she said. 'He told me he could spot a CP member a mile off. But you're butterflying from topic to topic. You did that when we first met in the café last September. Anyway, what about a drink soon? Or even a meal out. And what did you think of *The Eyes of Reason*?'

'It's amazing,' I said truthfully. 'Through the characters I felt the movement of history. They felt like real people in a real and history-changing situation. It is tragic, though, that two decades on, the socialist experiment in that country is in deep trouble.'

Shirley looked at me, nodding, making no comment. I didn't immediately take her up on her proposal for a meal or a drink somewhere, though was now regarding her as a friend with whom I would like to stay in touch.

35

In early March frost was about on several days in succession, and fog again arrived on the scene to accompany it. My windows at what was still my home were clouded in the mornings with moisture as well as dirt. A member of a revered pop music group and his wife were arrested for possession of cannabis. Even more sensationally, an American spacecraft succeeded in docking with another, named, in hope, 'a lunar module', and the main ship returned to earth, splashing down in the ocean somewhere.

Ann made appearances at the college, not always for all the time she was employed to do so. One day in that first week of the month her Canadian boyfriend looked into the staff room, saying he had an urgent message for her. 'She's teaching,' said Stanley Payne, before I could offer any useful thoughts. This might have been expected to encourage patience on the boyfriend's part, but, as we learnt later, he then went from classroom to classroom until he found her. Once located, Ann was compelled to abandon her business studies students to their own devices, and went off with him to the office she shared with Stanley and me, where they were interrupted by Stanley a few minutes later. They were then, he told me later, 'shouting the odds and going hammer and tongs'.

Stanley later prised from Ann the information that her boyfriend had been angry she had been meeting someone else without his knowledge, and had come down to the college 'to have it out' with her. Stanley, looking at me meaningfully, when he passed this on to me, said he had asked her: 'Did you say 'have it *out*?' She had confirmed this, he said, without showing any sign she realised that he had been pretending he had thought the last of the three words said might be '*off*'.

I couldn't help asking Stanley if the 'someone else' whom Ann was apparently seeing was her husband, back on the scene once more.

'I don't think so,' he said. 'I saw her yesterday afternoon leaving the premises with the new part time chap. Someone you know, I think.'

Oh, I thought, Alan. He doesn't waste time.

'Alan?' I queried blankly. 'I wouldn't have thought so. I expect they just walked to the station together.'

I could see Stanley was not persuaded. When I saw Ann later that day, I did not question her; but noticed her head moving nervously up and down, and her lower lip trembling. In her black boots and mini-skirt she cut a forlorn figure. She moved off to the ladies' cloakroom without seeing anyone she passed.

It was that day I heard news of Shirley's evening class Russian student, long lost to view by me, the man from the Soviet Trade Delegation based in Highgate. Shirley told me he'd been away for the weekend at the Delegation's country home in Kent, and when returning had a driving accident. He had been at the wheel. The vehicle had overturned. Shaken, Vladimir had accepted a drink from a bottle of whisky proffered by a passenger. When the police arrived, he was breathalysed and the test had, not surprisingly, proved positive for alcohol. Vladimir had to appear before the magistrates for driving under the influence of alcohol, and he was duly acquitted of guilt. 'Do you believe his story?' Shirley asked me.

Vladimir had not, however, turned up to the evening class that week. She had got the story from the press, not from the man himself.

'Have you considered the chances,' enquired Oliver, who was hovering nearby, 'that your Russian student could be a spy?'

'I suppose he could be,' came the rejoinder, 'but I doubt if my Monday evening class throws up many opportunities for sniffing out government and military information.'

'It would be a start,' said Oliver.

'But not a very good one.'

March meandered on. One Sunday, a windy, rainy and fresh day, I wandered down the Holloway Road to see what films were on at the local cinemas. Returning, unimpressed by the films advertised on the outside hoardings, I observed on the pavement at a road junction what looked like a trail of blood, a trail which went round the corner and then petered out. It was wet. I never found out the cause of the blood, if it was blood. For a second the thought of a gangland killing travelled wildly through my head, induced by the recent conviction and long custodial sentences for the Kray brothers, two notorious criminal underworld figures, for cold-blooded gangland murders. At that time the Kray killings were on the minds of many, after months of publicity for the trials.

But as I stood there, a conversation that, I imagined momentarily, might have a mysterious connection with the trail of blood I had just observed, was begun. A man in his forties, not well dressed, but confident, spoke to me.

'Well now, young man,' he said 'how would you like to win the football pools?'

I had no instant answer, but none was needed. He carried on an entirely unilateral discussion. He told me he had come close to winning, after working seven days a week for fifteen years. He said that if he had a few thousand pounds, he'd take two children out of an orphanage, give them an education, which he didn't have...and stop drinking.

I grinned at him and he grinned back. He'd been working that morning, he said. 'I'm the gaffer. I work for myself like. Earning their fucking wages for next week.'

Then he went on. 'I should have been a policeman and made a lot of money. Nine out of ten are crooked. Well, seven out of ten. They nicked the Krays, didn't they, Ronnie and Reggie. But nobody nicked the police....all that bribery and corruption.'

We were walking alongside each other and in silence. Then he said: 'Well, I wish you all the best, young man,' and crossed the road. I did not see him again. It was a very small fragment of a life, a minute or two only, which I had witnessed. And its connection with the trail of blood was, I decided, only in my head.

I visited Alan one evening at his rented home in Muswell Hill.

I had not seen anything of him for a while, the feeling having grown in me that he had not respected friendship boundaries enough in regard to my relationship with Marion. On his part he had no doubt been occupied with work and studies, but I was wondering too if he had been busy adding Ann Feldman to his list of conquests.

The large house in a tree-lined avenue was split into several flats, all approached by the central front door of the house. What seemed to me to be akin to a grand spiral staircase led the way to Alan's bedsit and kitchen on the first floor. To my surprise, his long suffering girlfriend, who told me she had a place of her own not far away, was present.

It occurred to me that he might prefer that she lived further away than she did. Yet they referred to each other as if they were a firmly established couple. Alan's girlfriend, however, said little, and did not demonstrate much happiness in her face. Alan was his usual chatty, relaxed and confident self. Male undergraduate humour still survived in him, as I saw when I visited the lavatory. A notice on the door informed me – 'Trespassers will be asphyxiated'.

This time we didn't talk about politics. Alan amused me by his description of witnessing Professor Schwarzenberger unusually at a loss, for once actually at the receiving end of a put-down. Alan had arrived outside a lift at Senate House when the Professor was persistently trying to gain the attention of the Head of Department or Dean of Faculty or somebody, who was already entering the lift and waving him away with the words 'Later, Georg, later'. The Professor, said Alan, had stood there even after the lift doors had closed, opening and shutting his mouth like a fish on automatic pilot. He had received a small dose of what he himself dished out in quantities. Justice had been done.

Alan's girlfriend only looked more despondent and, and after a short while, departed, saying she had things to do. Then it was that Alan told me they had decided to end their relationship, but with friendship continuing. 'Mutual decision?' I asked.

'Hers, but with tears,' he said harshly, 'especially as I didn't protest.' He may, who knows, have been feeling guilty.

'I've heard that break-ups which start out being friendly don't always end that way.'

'Well, I'm hoping.'

This was not said mechanically, but Alan seemed keener to flesh out his knowledge of recent events at East Ham. I told him the full story, as I knew it, about Martin's clash with the Principal over Gas Board discrimination in recruitment, about Shirley and the squatters' leader furore, and also about Shirley's argument with Oliver Price on the subject of colour and discrimination. I avoided mentioning Marion and Martine. Alan listened intently.

'The way you speak about these things,' he commented at the end, allows me to think that you have at last jumped down into the political arena.'

'I'm interested in people,' I retorted. 'I'd prefer them to be progressive, but I'm inquisitive about them anyway. We all have our limitations, don't we? Who knows, in the distant future, you for one may be tied to some managerial desk, denouncing lefties as trouble makers and obstacles to the nation's progress. You still might be a decent person.'

'I'd be a traitor,' he said flatly.

I asked Alan if he'd been at the small-scale demo near Claridges Hotel and at Grosvenor Square against President Nixon's visit at the end of February. I quoted a newspaper hoarding declaring: 'It's jail, jail for Nixon demo', as if it had been illegal to protest while walking in public.

'I was, and was lucky to avoid arrest. The police were grabbing people just for being there. One of my friends was arrested, treated roughly, and finished up with a jail sentence. The police lied in court about him.'

'There weren't that many of us there,' he went on. 'Hundreds, not thousands. On the other hand, there were thousands of police who were, in a manner of speaking, demonstrating against us and over-ready to use violence. Some of our people were out of control, but not many. The war crimes of Johnson and Nixon in Vietnam are a billion times worse than anything a few angry unarmed demonstrators can do. Nixon'll get his come-uppance. Give it time.' His prediction, of course, was to come true, and in a spectacular fashion, though not because of the Vietnam war.

Conversation then drifted before I asked Alan what he thought of my colleague Ann. He simply said:

'Woof!' and then shut down. I let the subject go, and asked, taking a breath, something else.

'Have you met Shirley Tait?'

Alan grunted a yes, and said nothing more about her. I heard some time later from Bob Hardy that Alan had tried to get on to intimate terms with Shirley, and had failed. As for

Alan's long suffering, and now former, girlfriend, I was told, as reliably, that silence, rather than friendship, followed their breakup.

★

Around that time I witnessed Oliver Price and Peter Dawlish, over tea in the staff room, poring over an advertisement in the *Times Educational Supplement*. The post on offer was that of Principal Lecturer in English at a college away from the capital, and I saw Peter Dawlish, pen in hand, ring one of the words and add an exclamation mark to the margin.

The advertisement, shown to me as if its contents contained just cause for its creative author to consider his or her position, and to proceed with immediate penance, because of incompetence in deploying the English language, read: 'Good academic qualifications and teaching experience in schools and colleges is required.' The 'is' was the word that had been ringed. 'They must be so desperate and anxious for a PL that they cannot produce a single sentence without an error of syntax,' said Dawlish. He said this forcibly, causing his bow tie, as grand as ever, to quiver.

The conversation between the pair, with me as listener to both, moved on, as it sometimes did, to the subject of our colleague Jack O'Neill. 'He spent the whole of last term on John Keats,' said Oliver. 'I've been teaching Keats to a similar class this term, and we've completed it with three weeks to go.'

I broke in at this point. 'I expect he has quite a fund of remarks to make en passant.'

Said Peter Dawlish: 'I expect he knows the biography of Keats better than the texts themselves.'

Then Oliver Price: 'And I would imagine that the majority of his comments are of a sexual nature. That may produce student hilarity but not necessarily top grade examination results.'

I asked if they regretted Jack's appointment as the number three of the English section.

206

'Well,' said Peter Dawlish, 'there were two dishy birds who applied, but…, anyway,' he seemed to correct himself, 'we have Shirley.'

'It's better as it is,' said Oliver Price. 'Consider what's happened to the law timetable over this last two terms.' He was referring, of course, to Ann Feldman's absences and inadequacies.

I didn't wish Ann to be the subject of yet more staff room character demolition, and asked idly if anything more was known of the Major's situation.

'I have it on good authority,' said Oliver Price, considering the diminishing size of his cigarette, 'that a Governors' meeting will be considering his resignation letter. There is the Major's view, supported by the union, that his supposed letter of resignation was not effective, not being in unqualified terms. There is also the other view. I have heard him say that if his resignation is treated as final, he may apply for his own post when advertised. Did you know' – suddenly he looked at me instead of at his cigarette – 'the Major made a bid last year to enlarge the scope for English teaching in the college?'

'I didn't know that. It sounds a bit odd.'

'The Major certainly went about it in a Majorish way,' said Price. 'He kicked off by sending me a note informing me that he believed there was scope for more English teaching, and requesting me to come to his room to discuss it on Thursday the whatever it was. I was busy then, but wrote back and said I would be free the following Monday, and looked forward to seeing him in my room at such and such a time.'

'He came?'

'He did. I showed him item by item that all the English teaching he had in mind was already being done. At the end he said jolly good and strode off, presumably intending to fix on another good cause to support.'

Grumbling resumed here and there about Mr. Pringle's tightness over expenses' entitlement. Stanley Payne expressed discontent when Pringle had vetoed payment of petrol expenses for a long day's teaching by him on a management training course at a south London venue. 'You'll just have to leave a little earlier in the morning and travel by public transport, I'm afraid,' Pringle had said. Bob Hardy had likewise been irritated when he had asked for the provision of a couple of thousand sheets of foolscap paper for a sociological survey project, and had been told that he could have the number required, but that the paper would be of a smaller size than requested. Bob had been incensed.

'The man's a total nonentity. He hides away in that room, with his desk in such a position that he doesn't have to face anyone who walks in. He'd be truly happy if someone locked him in the store room at nine and let him out at five. He'd be cock-a-hoop then that at least his fucking stationery was safe.'

'A slight exaggeration?'

'Not really.'

One afternoon I observed Bob invite one of his female sociology students, who had knocked on the annexe staff room door and asked to speak to him, into the room for a discussion. I presumed this was about one of her essays, which it probably was. This was uncommon liberality by a staff member. As I watched them, sitting side by side, the girl's legs crossed, Bob's legs stretched out, I recognised the girl as Mary, about whom Jack O'Neill had waxed so lasciviously some months before with reference to the whereabouts of her missing umbrella.

Mary, I could see, was not the slightest degree abashed by the experience of sharing a room with several teaching staff at their leisure. I saw her glancing round, and even detected what I thought might be an appraising look in my direction. Almost all of her attention, though, was given to Bob.

Their discussion finished, Mary got up, walking with poise towards the door. Jack O'Neill, who like me had been devoting eye attention to her, declaimed after she had left the room:

'There isn't a mark, not a sign of history on Mary's face. She is perfect. If I had let her in here, I would have been reluctant to let her leave. Yet I have to recognise that although I am sure she is generous, she has no reason to be grateful to me.'

His tone was gentle and admiring, not in the least sexually predatory. Bob lit his pipe and said nothing. He seemed self-absorbed. It was only later, much later, when I had ceased to work at the college and met Bob for a drink one evening, that he told me he had had 'a short and discreet affair' with Mary. He had been meeting her nearby with his car, and had more than once driven out with her to a desolate spot near the Woolwich Ferry crossing, he said, sometimes going across the river on the ferry boat to Woolwich for refreshment with her at an ABC tea shop. He had told Diane nothing, and she had not voiced any suspicions, though there had been, he admitted, more tension between them.

Mary, Bob told me, had, when they had exchanged a final goodbye to each other, said 'Thank you', to him, as if he had contributed to the completion of her preparations for life at the university where she had been accepted.

This was the moment when I could no longer hold back from asking the question which I had not dared for several months to put to him.

'Does Diane mind about Shirley?' I asked, regretting immediately that I had asked it, as Bob's face was set hard. Despite my temerity, he answered.

'She does. Foolishly, when I've been out and about with Shirley, I told Diane I was with Jack. But nothing's happened between me and Shirley. It's been platonic, and Shirley didn't know I'd been lying to Diane. But she does now.'

'I shouldn't have asked,' I said.

'I shouldn't have lied.'

Just as, following my East Ham appointment the previous summer, I had been shepherded around the college and shown the ropes by my departing predecessor (he of the many job applications and quality mimicry), so I did the honours similarly for my own replacement, but without attempting to impersonate anyone, famous or otherwise.

This young man wore, as I did, a dark pinstripe suit and had a serious, even deferential manner. He wore heavy round toed shoes and his briefcase seemed to amount almost to an item of his clothing. I showed him where he would sit in the little room I had shared for two terms with Stanley and Ann, and warned him that he might be lumbered with some of Ann's work whenever she had a bad patch. As I spoke with him, an image of my predecessor, the man in a hurry, came unsought into my head, and I recalled his induction advice as to how to integrate myself – 'Fill in registers well and teach to a mediocre level and they'll know you're one of them,' he had said. This, was, I thought, as patronising as it was cynical, and probably as applicable to its author as to a few of my colleagues. I declined to repeat it to my successor.

As I jumped up to gesture towards some books on the glass shielded shelves (their number had grown during my occupancy), he jumped up too, and when I got up to leave the room he rose instantly, clutching his briefcase. It was almost a case of mimicry. Later, after I had introduced him to Jack O'Neill as 'the new law man', and after the said 'new law man' had left us, Jack told me there was a stunning resemblance between the two of us, rather like that, he said, between the pigs and the men at the close of Orwell's *Animal Farm*.

In those final March weeks before my departure from both college and London life, it so happened that I repeatedly met the physical education teacher, Irene, in the corridors of the main college building, or in the staff common room there. It was Irene who, at the time of the American Presidential election, had innocently asked which of the candidates was a hawk and which a dove. Whenever we met we swapped smiles or paused for snatches of friendly conversation. I hadn't told Irene directly of my resignation from East Ham and of my move to Suffolk, but the grapevine would have informed her. Then one day, a few days before term ended, when we stopped to talk, just outside the main building entrance, Irene said to me the most personal thing she had said yet:

'I'm sorry you're leaving,' adding my Christian name (as I would have said then, or my forename, as I would be more likely to say now). Was it the first time she had addressed me as 'Clive'? In her late twenties, owning personality together with a face composed of flowers, and looking years younger, dark-haired Irene was enormously attractive in my eyes. She was also conversationally lively. I could not help but be flattered by her interest in me.

I replied immediately to her expression of regret that I was leaving with the daring remark that I would like to take her with me.

'You shouldn't say things like that,' Irene replied in a similar spirit, 'as I might take you up on it.'

'That would be a good reason for saying it,' I countered.

A certain point had been reached, and yet I wished to postpone the moment when Irene might either lead me on further, or shoot down my hope of closer involvement with her.

I was aware Irene was married, without children, but had no idea of the quality of the relationship between her and her husband. I took a chance.

'I've got an idea,' I said 'for what to say in a farewell note from you to your husband.'

'Go on then,' she said.

I could not read her facial expression, but her grey-green eyes were shining, and she had not retreated even half a step after the conversation had taken the turn it had.

"'Must rush darling,' I dictated. 'I'm running away with another man. I'll tell you more later. Love Irene. P.S. Please don't blame yourself.' Could it be fairer than that?"

As I uttered these words, Irene first laughed, then stopped abruptly.

'Are you just having a game with me?' she asked, uncertainly. 'Did you know I've left my husband?'

I hadn't known. This put a different complexion on things. Unsure whether comment was needed, I felt encouraged.

'I'm a free person, unmarried,' I said simply.

I had emerged from the witticism closet and looked at her. 'Seriously, Irene, I'd love to get to know you better.' She didn't answer for a few seconds. I had, however trite and unsuitable my words, without doubt made a decisive move. Marion was now an engaging if mixed quality memory from the past, where she would remain, while Shirley was surely unreachable, now and in the future.

'Let's not talk here,' said Irene. 'Are you free now?'

I was. 'I'll show you where I work. Have you ever been in the gym?'

I said not. 'I've got the keys.' She glanced down at the keys attached to her navy blue tracksuit trousers.

So we went down to the small sports hall on the ground floor of the tall building, and Irene opened up. She then locked the door from the inside, and gestured to the little office at one end. This had a large chair facing the doorway, by which she stopped, looking at me without a word.

For a while we talked. Irene had been leaning against a desk while I was seated, and then she moved to sit on a corner of the big chair, sharing it with me. I reached for her hand. After that things happened so quickly. Suddenly we were sharing more than the chair, but not so long after that Irene said she had to go. We had spoken little, and I had no idea whether she wished this short-lived but passionate encounter to be only a beginning.

'I'd like to go on seeing you, Irene,' I said. 'But I'll soon be in Suffolk.' I gave her one of the pretentious business cards with which I had equipped myself several months before, having added to it with my fountain pen the address and phone number of my new college in Suffolk. Irene gave me a contact telephone number too.

We kissed a last time. She would soon, she said, be physically moving out of her marital home.

When I arrived back at the little staff room in the annexe, Stanley looked at me closely. 'Your tie's not straight,' he said. 'You look as if you've had the cat's cream. Have you been at it with Ann?'

I must have looked confused, probably consolidating his suspicion by reddening, and said: 'What are you talking about?' before hurrying off.

On the penultimate day of the Easter term, I responded to a general summons to a departmental staff meeting set to commence at two o'clock. The students had been sent away for the afternoon in recognition of this. After the meeting, during which the tedium was torture for no more than half an hour, the old annexe building became quiet, save for those staff who were conversing, reading or simply vegetating, either in the staff room or in niche offices like mine.

The little pink-walled room I shared opened off the continuous corridor which right-angled its way into the pattern of a square besides providing entry to seven now empty classrooms and a good-sized cloakroom where student coats could be deposited. I sat yards away from Stanley Payne, who was idly turning over the pages of a text book on commercial studies, while I marked essays. Ann, Stanley had told me, was about somewhere.

Then without warning the door flew open and David Fawcett stopped short in the doorway.

'Would you two mind coming with me as witnesses?' he asked. There seemed to be no basis for refusal in the tone of his voice. No jollity either.

'What's this about?' asked Stanley.

'Something's going on in the students' cloakroom,' was the answer. 'I don't know what students are coming to. It's a cheek they're using it.'

Nothing more was said till we reached the door to the cloakroom of which Fawcett had spoken. The frosted glass embedded in the door impeded a view inside, but suggestive sounds were audible from within.

We paused for perhaps half a dozen seconds, startled into passivity, during which the sounds continued, making alternative explanations than the one guessed increasingly implausible.

Fawcett said, white-faced: 'Right,' and wrenched open the door to the cloakroom. Inside were a man and a woman. The man was underneath, trousers gathered in disarray around his ankles. He was lying on a beige duffle coat. The woman was on top, in a seated position. She wasn't wearing very much, but often – at least in Stanley Payne's view – didn't. It was Ann.

'Get out!' she said, with more volume, more decisiveness and more anger, than I had ever seen from her. 'Get out!' The man was silent.

Fawcett was silent too, immobile, gaping.

'Get out!'

I took the initiative and closed the door separating them from us.

We drifted back, the three of us, to my office base, Fawcett still speechless. It was Stanley who could not repress words.

'That is disgusting. At a place of work. She's a nymphomaniac. There's no other word for it.'

There was a pause.

'It was your friend with her, wasn't it? The lawyer-cum-sociologist?' He was looking at me.

'I fear so.' It was, indeed, Alan.

Just then, Bob Hardy waltzed into the room whistling, dispensing camaraderie. Swiftly aware of our bemused conditions, he stopped whistling.

'What's up?' he asked breezily.

'Ann and your leftie sociology part-timer. At it like rabbits in the students' cloakroom.'

This was from Stanley. Fawcett was still in silent shock.

Bob seemed about to laugh, then contained himself, and said:

'Is it so dreadful? The students had gone, they thought they were in a private place...'

Fawcett finally said something: 'It's totally immoral. She's married.'

Bob rejoined: 'But hardly cohabiting with her husband. Can't you consider it in a robust, common sense way? It's not as if he was spanking her with a rolled up copy of *World Marxist Review*,' he went on without a glimmer of a grin. 'The one with the red cover.'

Fawcett reeled back against the corridor wall, traumatised by what he had seen, perhaps uninfluenced by Bob's frivolous fantasy.

'You think we should hush it up?' he said faintly.

'If you don't,' said Bob firmly, 'the department will get a lot of adverse publicity. And there's a high risk that you will be accused by Ann, backed up by Alan, of being a peeping tom.'

'There's that,' said Fawcett. There was a long pause. 'Is this place primarily for sexual trysts,' he said, looking at me, 'or an educational establishment?'

For a moment I thought he must know about my goings-on with Irene in the gym as well.

I contented myself with a reflective: 'There's something in what Bob says.'

Fawcett seemed beaten down by the whole experience. 'I may be making a big mistake,' he said, 'but I'll say nothing to Mr. Pringle.'

Then amazingly, he cracked a joke. 'It's not boys will be boys so much as lawyers will be lawyers.' Again, he looked at me as if he knew that I was similarly guilty, if not yet exposed to the world. I surmised that he had not yet recovered from the bruising he had taken over the Ron Bailey affair. He needed to avoid sustaining another blow to his authority and confidence.

So the matter was laid to rest. I was reminded of Snow's *The Sleep of Reason*, opening as it did, with a Vice-Chancellor's decision to send students down for having sex almost openly on University premises. Action against staff of a London technical college for comparable activity was thus avoided by 'the little shit's' agreement to keep the matter under wraps.

36

The day of my leaving came. I walked up the Holloway Road to the tiny station a last time. Frost sparkled on the wooden footbridge and on the platform and even on the sides of the rails. It was a beautiful morning. Overall a perfect symbol for winter's retirement from the scene and for my own retirement from East Ham. After not much more than half a year.

It was a day of pleasant partings. The genial and gentlemanly 'Liberal Studies but Hopeless' Herbert told me he would like to shake me by the hand, and that the college in Suffolk would be a place of less hustle and bustle.

'And of fewer sexual shenannigans,' I said to myself, participating loyally in an informal staff room pact not to tell Herbert about Ann and Alan's cloakroom dalliance, in case another stroke or heart attack might be visited upon him. I hazarded an equally private guess that, in Suffolk, day release apprentices would not roar out that an intruder should have the door shut in his face in quite the way Herbert, officially in charge and in front of the class, had recently experienced.

About my Suffolk future, Herbert also said, with a smile: 'You'll have to learn the language, of course.'

Bob Hardy was less up-beat. 'It's a great escape,' he said. 'You've tunnelled out under the wire. But for how long before you have to do it again? Good luck, anyway. I'm jealous.'

I had been told there would be a gathering in the large staff room at twelve noon and so there was. One other staff member was leaving. There was a small present for each of us, the result of a collection organised conscientiously by Peter Dawlish. I was astonished to receive anything, my sojourn at the college having been so short. I felt I deserved nothing. But a fountain pen came my way. I now had two, to match the number of my suits. Michael Hastings came up to me, pipe puffing, and told me I should find it easier to buy a house in East Anglia than in London. I forbore from asking what his was worth now, and Bob, standing by, had the decency to avoid broaching the subject too.

Reg, 'Mr. Register', came over and in his shrill, harsh voice thanked me in a heartfelt way for my 'commendable register maintenance' on the municipal accountancy courses. 'No entry errors, that I could see,' he said, and I took it that he had looked very rigorously. If I had been a Battle of Britain fighter pilot, returning to base after downing a dozen Messerschmitts, there to be thanked emotionally by the Air Minister on behalf of the people of Britain, I could not have felt more highly praised.

I was tempted to apologise to Peter Dawlish for having dismissed him mentally as the self-important snob characterised once by Bob Hardy, though I should have found more tactful wording had I gone ahead. In any event the temptation diminished after he had recited, in lighter hearted mood than usual, two limericks, far from risqué. Both relied on awkward rhymes and a largely unsuccessful struggle to be effective comedy. He said farewell in a well-meaning way. I was beginning to think I had under-estimated his good qualities, especially as he had been lately without self-importance in expressing anger over the circumstances of his abortive application for the senior post in another college – advertised, as he had announced critically at the time, with flagrant disregard for a grammatically essential plural word. At his interview, just days previously, he had been incensed by the deferential attitude of the head of department towards that college's chief.

'It was just rampant arse-licking,' he declared, reminding me of the firm Marion worked for, and had told me about, a powerful company 'full of crawlers'. He had, he said, withdrawn and walked out, with as much politeness as he could muster, before the end of the interview. So he was, as I was learning, capable of being anti-Establishment in his own way when the occasion justified it. On the other hand he told me that in my rural Suffolk estate, I would be able to shout 'Ho, Varlet!', and have my bidding done routinely by my serfs. His bow tie was askew, as he said this, and he thanked me for pointing this out, retreating promptly to a mirror to correct its position. I examined it surreptitiously a final time when adjusted: it seemed smaller, less grand than it had been in my head.

Oliver Price had forgotten I was leaving, but on being reminded, said farewell to me in a courteous manner. Ann Feldman walked into the staff room, as if by accident, during the leaving ceremonial. She looked bewildered, as if she too had forgotten anyone was leaving. Her bewilderment, as Jack O'Neill might have said, was a metaphor for her life. There was no sign of her awareness of the greater notoriety she had lately generated, for the word about her cloakroom performance with Alan had travelled quickly through whispered confidences among some of my colleagues, in spite of David Fawcett's injunction to 'keep it dark'. Martin, liberal studies Martin, had not been told, to avoid expressions of horror on his part, and perhaps never was told. I said goodbye to him, expressing great respect for his lone campaign against racism by the Gas Board, and feeling his own embarrassment as I spoke.

Shirley came into the staff room soon after Ann, and then came straight up to me. 'I shall miss your company,' she said, adding, very quietly with her lovely smile, 'and opportunities to recruit you.'

I laughed at this. Then Bob Hardy came in to the room, his face animated. 'I've been elucidating Keynesian economics to the municipal treasurers and accountants,' he said to several of us. 'I explained how public expenditure, including Nazi Germany's investment in attacking other countries and building gas ovens, extracts capitalist countries from slumps. It was off the top of my head. I don't think they quite understood the drift of my exposition, but it was probably my fault for being badly prepared.'

I asked, straight-faced: 'Did you link this, for example, to how Reg's hand-held calculators can be used for Keynesian purposes in a municipal accounting context? Wouldn't that have given your propositions more direct relevance?'

Bob's response to this wretched attempt at humour was jovial. 'Do you want me to stuff a calculator up your...?' He left the final word unstated, and exchanged glances with Shirley. I had the impression that if they had fallen out over Bob's untruths to Diane, the position between them may by now have been resolved. He was certainly on good form at that moment.

He moved away as Messrs. Pringle and Plummer approached to say goodbye to me and the other leaver. I had hardly had the occasion to say hello to Plummer over the past two terms. So goodbye seemed an odd thing to say to him. I made the shortest possible thank you and goodbye speech, during which Jack O'Neill was writing furiously – goodness knows about what – on one corner of a table.

'How are things at home?' I asked him, as the gathering dispersed. 'There was a rumpus last night,' he said. 'Sally tore up my teaching copy of *Sons and Lovers*. But at least the court case has been dropped. This morning she was hitting me with an umbrella.' He had fresh scars on his hands.

I asked how his teaching was going and he told me he was getting more and more irresponsible. 'I'm only holding on to it by an effort of will. It's all very boring. What keeps me going is thinking of Thomas.' It was as desperate a mood as I had seen in him, although I had no doubt he would rise up again.

He demonstrated this the very next moment, saying: 'After early morning horrors, I arrive here, and what am I confronted with but three impossibly desirable fillies in the classroom.' Once more, ecstasy in his face and voice. Shirley was not close enough to reprove him.

There was no sign of the Major, who had finally been told that his half-intended resignation had been accepted, and that his employment at the college was now at an end.

For him there was to be no ceremonial opportunity for goodbyes or a presentation.

Stanley Payne came up to me and told me he'd enjoyed conversation with me during 'my holiday' at the college.

The day after these farewells, Irene returned my call, as I'd been hoping she would. She proposed that we meet in central London for lunch and a walk. I agreed instantly. She also said that she did not know where what was between us was going, but that she wanted to know me more. I reciprocated. So we did get to know each other better, and in fact that was far from the end of it.

Rounding up

My Suffolk phase began. My removal required trips to Ipswich by train, laden with suitcases. My landlady said, without enthusiasm, that she would miss me and so would her cats. For my part I did miss her cats, though not to the point of wallowing in depression.

A few weeks after my departure I heard, first from Bob Hardy, then from Alan, of sea changes in their respective domestic situations. Bob was extremely angry with Alan. He had, as he had done with me, invited Alan round for a meal with himself and Diane, and was not long afterwards told by Diane that she was involved with Alan. Alan had taken advantage of Bob's long-standing neglect of her.

Alan had been seeing enough of Diane for Bob to punch him on the nose during a drunken exchange of views in the Denmark Arms, causing the ejection of both from the premises, and the ejection of Bob from the home he had shared with Diane. Alan accepted his punishment, and did not report Bob to the police. Nor did Bob, rejecting the precedent set by a student the previous autumn by reporting Mr. Patience the caretaker to police for intimidating words which he had answered with a blow to Mr. Patience's nose, report Alan similarly for provoking him by his behaviour with Diane.

Visiting London soon after this, I dared to ask Bob if his friendship with Shirley had played a part in the rupture with Diane. He said it had, although Shirley had made it crystal clear early on that she did not go beyond platonic friendship with married men.

Not so long after the punch on the nose, Alan replaced Bob in Diane's home, and soon after that – it did not altogether surprise me – Bob and Shirley became a couple too. And within a year Bob succeeded in making his own escape from the college.

I did not stay in touch with Martin – self-contained, pedantic in manner, but wholly honest, brave, and honourable – who had been prepared to challenge racist recruitment practice by the Gas Board in the press, and then face bad-temper and racism from Principal Plummer. Dai Griffths, the liberal studies chief, it may be said, soon secured a head of department's post on the other side of London.

What became of the Major after his exit from the college remained unknown to me, and even to Stanley Payne, who had been his chief ally. In retrospect I should have felt more sympathy for the Major. It was too easy to think of him as a caricature of an army officer, as a comic figure, rather than a tragic person, who had fought bravely in the war (as Stanley had done), was drinking too much, and whose post-army career in further education might, after his untidy departure, be impossible to resurrect.

In the summer, I heard, Peter Dawlish married his fiancée, and a year or so after that he found a teacher training college that would recruit him to its ranks, together with his wine-coloured corduroy jacket and bow tie, or fresh versions of these items. About the same time Jack O'Neill told me that Ann had left the college, and had got married for the second time, not to her Canadian boyfriend, but to the manager of a public house in Romford. There, it was said, she was helping her husband behind the bar, and seemed much more fulfilled pulling pints – and, Stanley Payne would have suggested, customers – than she had been teaching students.

Stanley, Martin, Michael Hastings and 'Mr. Register', as may well be imagined, continued to be part of the college furniture – as did a dissatisfied David Fawcett, despite his energetic and repeated attempts to gain promotion elsewhere.

Not many years later Oliver Price died of a sudden heart attack. He too had stayed at the college, never gaining more seniority there or elsewhere, despite persistent efforts on his part to better himself.

Alan kept his part time East Ham appointment, and was, before long, given additional work. Once he gained his master's degree (it was mainly, he said, 'a question of surviving the Professor Schwarzenberger experience'), he secured a university teaching post.

Alan and Diane are still together, with children and even one grandchild, while Bob and Shirley also remained a couple, though without offspring themselves, something I am sure both regretted, but accepted. Less tolerant of Bob's waywardness than Diane had been, Shirley compelled Bob to defer to her more than he had done to Diane: they proved to be a remarkably well suited pair. I have stayed in touch with them across the years, during which I have read for a second time – after a long interval – Stefan Heym's *The Eyes of Reason*. I found it again powerful, moving and memorable (if too long) – as well as anti-Nazi and, but not simplistically, pro-communist. Sententious Snow's *The Sleep of Reason* is not a patch on it.

While Alan, in recent years, I am told, has been a Green Party member, Bob and Shirley both remained 'old-fashioned socialists', and despaired of the policies implemented by successive governments, Conservative and Labour. They participated, of course, in the great anti-Iraq war demonstration in 2003, in which Alan, and even I added to the numbers marching. 'The chances of the world going up in flames are growing, not diminishing,' Shirley would say as distant war succeeded distant war, and I know she – and Bob – are as busy as ever today in encouraging opposition to the policies of the present Conservative-Liberal government.

I kept in touch with Jack O'Neill, whose family difficulties never went away, but were reduced as Thomas grew older. Not long after I moved to Suffolk, Jack told me, during a phone call, that Sally had visited the college, rampaging her way along many corridors, peering into many classrooms, seeing everyone from Mr. Plummer to Mr. Patience the caretaker, all for the purpose of winning support for her campaign to stop Jack from going to lectures for which he had registered at the French Institute. She had been no more successful than when she had visited Home Secretary Callaghan's office to demand guarantees that she would be free from future arrest.

Jack carried on at East Ham, never gaining promotion and never aggrieved by the fact, till retirement. Sally never threw off her mental illness, though in latter years was less turbulent in her doings than formerly. The relationship between the couple, though volatile, was inexplicable to me. When I walked with them once to a pub in Crouch End, Sally claimed that the tavern concerned was nasty, common and vulgar. Jack had retorted: 'Do you mean we've been thrown out of it?' She had not appreciated the wit.

Only recently, following Jack's death not many months after that of Sally (to whom he had remained incorrigibly loyal to the end), I attended a memorial service for him. One of those attending the event (which was far more of a celebration than a service), had recalled a crisis moment, belonging to years during which I had lost touch with Jack, when he had been anxiously preoccupied with her doings of the moment. 'She's on the south coast, robbing banks – and with a green plastic water pistol in my name,' Jack had claimed. The 'in my name' had been theatrically stressed.

During the celebration, little Thomas, now in early middle age, paid tribute to his father, with whose love and support (and resort to a private boarding school), he had safely reached adulthood. 'He walked me through it.' These are words that will remain with me, as will the sharp recollection of his father's vital personality. Jack O'Neill had the heart of the matter in him, if needing to be reproved frequently for breaches of not yet fully formulated rules of political correctness regarding women in his impromptu commentaries.

Now is the time for me to return to the drab tasks of the day. When I have attacked these, I may turn to the newspaper or the television. I have escaped from my end-of-line college prisoner-of-war camp, unless retirement is just another kind of incarceration. My house is worth, at latest valuation, far, far more than Michael Hastings ever claimed for his own home, so if he is still alive, he must be sitting on a gold mine too. The newspapers tell me house prices are falling. He wouldn't have liked that.

If I dally still about becoming engaged more actively with the problems of the world, I have nailed my colours to the mast in one respect. After illuminating my memories from reading my diary of the time at East Ham, I decided that this ageing piece of memorabilia had served its purpose. To use Thomas Carlyle's magisterial words, I have edited it by fire. It is no longer possible for me to pass from memory to diary and from diary to memory, to resolve any doubt as to the accuracy of details. My journal is now dust and ashes.

I have not troubled to count the number of fragments of lives this memoir contains. There are, I know, rather a lot. The jury will tell us whether I made the right decision in continuing with this untidy, idiosyncratic project to its peaceful conclusion.

It is now time for me to sit down at dinner with Irene. Amazingly, and lovingly, we are still together, and still close to our two children. At this end moment, composer Alan Bush's *The Sugar Reapers alias Guyana Johnny* crosses my mind. I wonder if one day it will reach the London Coliseum or even the Royal Opera House.

December 2010   Clive Bates